Further Praise for *We Come*

"I read Odie Lindsey's *We Come to Our Senses* in a way that books rarely compel me to: thinking I'll spend an hour (evening was upon me and this particular book was going to stir up thoughts of war), and before I think to rise again from my chair it is finished and I have to find a clock to understand how late it actually is. Not only compulsively readable, the thoughts these war stories stirred were rich and complex and heartening in their universal humanity. This is a remarkable collection by a splendid new writer."

—Robert Olen Butler, Pulitzer Prize winner
and author of *A Good Scent from a Strange Mountain*

"The war is over, but it's just the beginning for Lindsey's characters in this gritty and ambitious debut collection. The heat is suffocating in the Deep South; there are few jobs and a limited pool of friends, but the TV works just fine and there are plenty of guns to shoot when the bars close at midnight. The true gift here is the prose. Odie Lindsey is an innovative and consummate prose stylist."   —Mary Miller,
author of *The Last Days of California*

"The debut we hope for: heart-quickening, kinetic, relentless in its engagement with our time."   —Paul Yoon,
author of *Snow Hunters*

"The impact of the stories derives from Lindsey's ability to assume a convincing voice."   —*Charlotte Observer*

"With a searing insightfulness and a dark humor all his own, Odie Lindsey holds up a powerful lens to an experience of modern American warfare that has been largely ignored in fiction— that of female veterans. This is a collection about how the battles we wage with the external world are really only half the fight."
—Bonnie Jo Campbell, National Book Award finalist and author of *Once Upon a River*

"Brutal, precise, like a bullet to the heart, Lindsey's prose is exactly right for conveying what war does to the human soul. Whether comic or tragic, the characters in these stories feel so vibratingly alive they seem to be whispering directly into your ear."
—Helen Benedict, author of *Sand Queen* and *The Lonely Soldier*

"Here's an exciting, even thrilling new voice I'm delighted to read, to hear in my head. He's got all the notes, he's all in. Odie Lindsey's a terrific writer—pitch-perfect, entirely under control at high speed—who doesn't hold anything back."
—Brad Watson, author of *Aliens in the Prime of Their Lives*

"The writing here is nuanced, correct, and felt enough that, for once, 'Support Our Troops' is not political pablum. One might say that in Odie Lindsey's care, 'Support Our Troops' is a literary imperative."
—Padgett Powell, author of *Cries for Help, Various*

"A dark, sometimes funny, and certainly complex collection of stories."
—*The Rumpus*

WE
COME TO
OUR
SENSES

STORIES

ODIE LINDSEY

W. W. NORTON & COMPANY | NEW YORK | LONDON

INDEPENDENT PUBLISHERS SINCE 1923

"Evie M." published in the *Iowa Review*, reprinted in *Best American Short Stories 2014*. "So Bored in Nashville" in *Southern Cultures*. "Clean" in *Fourteen Hills*. "They" in *You Must Be This Tall to Ride*. "Hers" in *Forty Stories: New Writing from Harper Perennial*.

For information about permission to reproduce selections from this book, write to Permissions, W. W. Norton & Company, Inc., 500 Fifth Avenue, New York, NY 10110

For information about special discounts for bulk purchases, please contact W. W. Norton Special Sales at specialsales@wwnorton.com or 800-233-4830

Manufacturing by LSC Communications Harrisonburg
Book design by Brooke Koven
Production manager: Louise Mattarelliano

Library of Congress Cataloging-in-Publication Data

Names: Lindsey, Odie, author.
Title: We come to our senses : stories / Odie Lindsey.
Description: First edition. | New York : W. W. Norton & Company, 2016.
Identifiers: LCCN 2016008755 | ISBN 9780393249606 (hardcover)
Subjects: LCSH: Veterans—Fiction. | Southern States—Fiction. |
GSAFD: Psychological fiction. | War stories.
Classification: LCC PS3612.I53568 A6 2016 | DDC 813/.6—dc23
LC record available at https://lccn.loc.gov/2016008755

ISBN 978-0-393-35419-5 pbk.

W. W. Norton & Company, Inc.
500 Fifth Avenue, New York, N.Y. 10110
www.wwnorton.com

W. W. Norton & Company Ltd.
15 Carlisle Street, London W1D 3BS

1 2 3 4 5 6 7 8 9 0

FOR NANCY RUSSELL

But, ultimately, what have you got against
aphrodisiacs?

—J. BAUDRILLARD
The Gulf War Did Not Take Place

CONTENTS

Evie M.

TODAY I PHONED and had a cup of coffee, created/ distributed a handful of B-20s, then phoned and had a cup of coffee. We ran out of powder creamer, but there were creams from McDonald's in the break area mini-fridge, which I just disinfected. Around 4:40 I decided to cruise hyperlinks until close of business. There was something about our President, and news that a small plane had crashed somewhere in Illinois. A sullen pop diva will guest-star on a Thursday night prime-time. It's sweeps. Her crimson lips were parted in the photo, and for an instant I couldn't help but picture myself ejaculating—I guess. Accurate or not, I felt despicable, and quickly went to scrub my hands. I must remember to remember her name, to purchase her recordings. I drove home.

HOME, where the shows are on. Between five-thirty and seven: utter contentment. The reruns allow me to nod off for a few, and then rejoin any story, anytime, without worry. They showed us these same shows in the female barracks' dayroom, and in the females' Quonset at the marshaling base, and you could even watch them at forward ops (where we shared the rec tent with the men). Usually a nap, followed by a quick Swiffer-sweep of the apartment, will help me to unwind, before the new episodes come on at seven. I know everything, until the new episodes come on, at seven.

Only, today, someone has called and the red light blinks. No one ever calls. I am terrified to check the message, so I do not, and then do not sleep.

BACK to work. Somebody left the coffee machine on all night, so the break area smelled burnt and the pot had a veneer of tar-stuff on the bottom. I picked it up and looked into it, considered scrubbing it, considered smashing it into the brushed-steel sink, my knuckles grinding the shards, but then put it back and trod down the long hall to another break area, where I poured a cup. There were pyres everywhere in the desert. There was plenty of powder cream, here. Near my partition a thin clerk shrugged his shoulders at the scorched pot. The back of his khakis were wrinkled from having been worn too many times without a wash. I told him about the other break area, but he just stared at me. I told him there was plenty of cream.

Later, my supervisor stood at the edge of my work space and flashed his perfect, glazed teeth. It made me nervous, which I think he enjoyed. Enjoys. He's younger than I am but doesn't act it. He told me he's been listening in on my customer calls, and that I needed to Master the Art of Inflection.

Told me that I had a lovely voice, but that if I didn't sound interested in our product, I could not expect anyone else to get interested in it. Could I? Huh?

At lunch, my hands and face were filmy from a French dip. I finished half of it before I had to rush to the women's room to wash. There was only an air-dryer, so I used toilet paper to pat myself, and ended up with tissue pills all over my chin. After that, I drove to McDonald's for coffee. I asked the woman for a handful of extra creams and she glared at me as if I were the cause of something awful, like a tumor. She spoke into a headset, then slammed the window. As I pulled away my exhaust made a grumbling sound, like rocks tumbling in a pipe, like the collision of track gears on an M113A3 personnel carrier. I simply cannot afford any extra expenses, car repair or anything. I put the car in park and sat in the lot, rubbing my thumbs against the corrugated thimbles of cream, rubbing and rubbing until another headset person knocked on my window and ordered me away.

Supervisor came by, again. He stood over my shoulder, breathing through his nose. At some point I had to turn and look up at him. His smile, the clinical porcelain of his incisors, made me feel like a schoolgirl humiliated by her teacher. (In elementary, I was given remedial tooth-brushing lessons after the red, plaque disclosure pill polluted my mouth.) The Art of Inflection, Evie, he said to me again. He then squeezed my neck, kneaded it and walked off. I spent the rest of the day refreshing my in-box. Someone sent a joke email that showed a fat cartoon woman in black lingerie. Her beet-red nipples were spilling over the top, and her vagina was bisected by the panties. A stick-thin bald man dressed in only an undershirt, and with a small, limp cock, said that Victoria's secret was out: models were one thing, but nobody's *wife* looks good in these outfits. It wasn't funny. I sent it on to my account reps.

THE red light was a message from Helen—I finally checked, I had to sleep. We broke up because she took a job elsewhere. Maybe this wasn't the end of the world, but it wasn't so god-damn good either. The thing is, we sat Indian-style on the wooden floor in her empty living room, the window light gentle and lemony, the moving trucks already gone, and she promised that *she* would hang in there if *I* hung in there.

I have to stop thinking about it, her, now. If you heat an individual serving (two) of Rich's frozen glazed donuts for between twenty-nine and forty-two seconds they'll be as hot and fresh as fresh. We had this little bitch dog in the desert, this black-and-white mutt that found us, just wandered into camp out of nowhere. We fed it chunks of dehydrated pork patty and whatever from our MREs, and someone named it Sheeba, that name my god I hated that name. Growing up I'd never been allowed to have a dog, so I gave it every leftover from my meal packet, gum and salt and powdered cream and everything, and it began to sleep under my cot every night, and I'd dangle my hand down there on her ribs for as long as I could stay awake, and . . . And you'd pat it, her, Sheeba, and puffs of dust would fly from her fur it was so funny so dirty, and once she was outside the compound berm, out there in the sand, pawing at a beetle, springing back from a tiny bug or something, crouching on her front paws and growling at it like she was a puppy, and a few of us laughed and then went in the tent and some guys from the motor pool took bets and shot it. Her. It depends on how frozen the donuts are. You can tell they are ready when they are spongy but not hard as the tines of your fork test them. Then: stop. Any longer in the microwave and the dough seizes up, and the glaze will coagulate. I know this.

SUPERVISOR'S teeth are actually only clean on the front. He uses those grocery-store whitening strips instead of going to the dentist. I want to tell him about his yellow side-teeth. Wanted to tell him today when he smiled and told me to remember—told me twice—that Annual Evaluations are upon us.

I was sitting on the floor next to the copier when he said this. I can't bear it when the copier spool gets dry because of too much usage. It's precarious, because you'd think you could just relubricate the plate glass with a wipe of oil, like greasing a cookie sheet. But you absolutely can*not* put an abundance of copier oil on it, or it won't feed right. Just a film, a light au jus. Unfortunately, if you're out of copier oil and still have to bundle stapled and sorted sets of product logs for supervisors with white front teeth, you know that this will take your entire day: press the green button, get through (at best) one set, deal with the jam. Repeat repeat repeat. Empty Duplicator. Replace Last Two Originals In

Document Feeder. Repeat repeat repeat. Close Document Feeder. Repeat. It kills you after about an hour or so. Finally, you just sit on the floor, dying over the fact that if you wait for the repairman to arrive and relubricate, your ass is over. Annual Evaluations are here.

HOME again, though I can't seem to break from work. The D-20 is for requisition and the B-20 is for back order and the Service Order is for the copy machine and the T-sheet is for time off and the PTO sheet is for paid time off and the P-sheet is for parts order and the O-sheet is for order-in-stock. I've seen this episode a thousand times. I know all the dialogue by heart. Helen called again and her voice is . . . She hopes I'll call her back, hopes I'm still talking to the counselor woman at VA. The box says that in seven and one-half minutes my sirloin steak will be perfect. Yet I know the mashed potatoes will be icy in the middle. It will take a precise balance of extra microwave and stirring to get them just warm enough to eat without completely ruining the steak itself. I realize at about six minutes in that I am going to kill myself. At seven minutes, I determine that I will not die with the guilt of making anyone feel bad. I must start writing my notes.

The potatoes are not done. The extra minute ruins the sirloin.

> FATHER—
> *I cannot begin to describe how sorry. My action is*
> *against everything you believe, and I know . . . I*

think of your lifetime behind the desk, in the office.
Honor and strength and poise—and you never once
complained. I love and envy you. I am not strong. I
am not obliged. I am not . . .

Jesus Christ, the shows are on.

YOU must adore digital cable. The search options have revolutionized me and everybody. Technology marches, no matter. You can be groped inside the hot metal gut of a troop carrier, or you can see things die and see pieces of dead things. I promise you it will not affect the remote control. Though I forgot to write down the name of the pop singer, with digital cable I can see into the future, and I will find her. This is amazing. She will come back to me.

SUPERVISOR *yelled* at me today. So close I could smell his cologne. He barked that I wasn't "into it" the way I needed to be. Sandalwood. As consequence I couldn't finish my first note, to my father. What if everyone counted on someone else to locate the clerical errors?, Supervisor demanded. What if everyone produced reports whose pages crinkled because of a stupid copy jam? What if the whole damn order of things broke down?

Before he escorted me into his office, I was thinking about the salty taste of frayed baseball glove. After the Little League coach lets you on the team but still won't play you—save once, two innings in right field—things get quiet. In the corner of the dugout, wrapped in chain-link, your cleats sucking into mud and mangled seed husks, sometimes you chew on the leather strips that welt your glove. Dad realized things about me real early, and he showed me how to field with two hands, how to keep my elbow up when I was batting, and above all how to always run over and back up the throw on any given play. We knotted my hair under my ball cap. He said hustle was supreme, beyond even talent or background, and told me I could get past anyone's expectation of who or what I was supposed to be, if I could just keep up the hustle. So I was going to revise my note to him from those principles of ambition, of compassion. Conviction. I want Dad to know that I believed in them, that I learned.

Inside the supervisor's office is an L-shaped hardwood desk and a plastic *Ficus benjamina* tree in a dark wicker pot. He has no windows, but he does have three titanium-white walls and a white drop-ceiling and fluorescent overheads, and one glass wall that faces the general office. On the wall behind his desk is a diploma for business administration, alongside a membership certificate of Sigma Alpha Epsilon, and a Kiwanis Club award and a Young Entrepreneurs of Birmingham Intramural Softball group photo. As he screamed I stared past him, to those certificates—at least until he yelled the words "copy machine," at which point I made the mistake of snapping into focus. I then remembered my baseball glove, and realized how fucked everything was. He says they're also going to check and see who's doing what online, and deal with that, pronto. He left the mini blinds open and the office could see everything. I thought of Helen, who, when she worked here, would have been waiting for me in the break area. I guess he saw my eyes start to water, because he eased his tone, and said something about everybody's respecting my time in the service and all, etc. This prattle allowed me to again focus on the certificates. I have got to finish my notes immediately. I have got to finish my notes.

HELEN called my house four times. She's coming into town this week and *Really wants to see me* and says I *Need to stop worrying*, etc. Her box-dye auburn hair is dry to the touch. Her eyelids sag and have tiny folds. I wonder if I should add her to my list of notes? Dad, Mom, Carla and Ray, and Helen. Maybe. What can I say? Can I say that she shouldn't worry about those road-to-nowhere veins on her legs? That I feel like I'm breathing under the ocean when she's around? I don't know. *Just call me back*, she says. The shows are on in seven minutes and I've got a broccoli and cheddar that must sit for 120 additional seconds before the cellophane can even be removed.

MOTHER—
How difficult for you. Chocolate milk on the yellow
sofa? Sabotaged cotillion? But you taught me so much.
I'm sorry I was. I am proud at least that you would
be proud of my home. Perhaps you can . . .

HEART-RED, quivering sun on white talc sand. Crimped emerald blade of fern. Chocolaty plowed earth. Ice-sheet blinding, sun-lit snow traversed by knotted tree shadow. Salty gray ocean smashes rocky shore in fall.
The phone on my desk rings. I pray it is Helen. I answer,

and our West Coast rep yells that I was supposed to get a boxful of promos to Brendel's, then asks where the hell they are. I tell him that I sent them two-day; he calls me a dumbass for not overnighting. I tell him that the *Employees' Handbook* says No Overnight Packages Are To Be Sent unless either (A) an error has been made by the supplier's (our) end of things, thus causing a delay in shipment, or (B) the recipient provides their personal shipping account code for forward billing. He tells me that I should fuck the *Employees' Handbook*, because, as I very well know, Brendel's sells approximately 29 percent of all of our merchandise to all of the United-fucking-States, and that if product sales and revenue and placement like that is not important enough for overnight promos, he'll suck my dick. We fall silent. Seconds later he says, Well, you get my point anyways, Evie, and then tells me he's calling my supervisor, and hangs up.

These phrases are no kind of note for Helen. I'd been looking at the nature photos of my screen saver, desperate to list something pure.

THE thing is, was, Helen and I sat Indian-style on that glazy wood floor, the window light gentle and lemony. The house was clean and bright and empty. We stared at each other, and into our own laps, her thumb and index finger gently kneading my knuckles. And that's when the memories blitzed the surface. I had never told her about the war. I'd been going so long with the men down inside me. For years I'd been shoving them into my gut, hustling past them best I could. Yet it, they, were all there again, their hands, their sweat, their greed. In memory, I had even sought their comfort, when my unit first arrived in-country, when missiles sliced the sky. At first, at marshaling, the terror had driven me to abandon myself to them. When all there was on the horizon was death.

I trembled. Helen scooted over to me. As her hand slid over my back, I realized that the episode would be so easy for her to dispatch. I understood then that the shame was only mine, the terror and ritual, and that Helen would embrace it, and take it, and send it off in a truck. All I had to do was confess.

Yet I just couldn't break the habit of keeping. The past stayed clogged inside my throat, just there. Here, now. I'm addicted to rerunning this scene.

ON the way in to work the gravelly sound beneath my car broke into a roar. The front end shook and the gas pedal mudded. I made it into the lot, hazards flashing, and told my supervisor I had to take it to the dealership service shop immediately. (Only the dealership service shop requires annual certification of every mechanic.) He said this was not a company problem, and that I had to do it on my own time. I called him sir, and reminded him that the dealership service shop would not be open on my own time until Saturday, and that I was sure the car wouldn't make it that long. He told me that I should look for a ride from a coworker. Or rent a car.

I had to sit down. I had to sit down as he took the last of the coffee from our station and then walked away, leaving the empty pot spitting on the machine. I could almost *feel* myself on the shoulder of the tar-stinking road, choking on the emissions of commuters, all of them able to get home and watch the shows. I can't stomach the hot smells of anyone else's car. I won't ride in someone else's baby-seated, taco-wrappered, cola-ringed, faded-upholstery, dust-caked vehicle. And my rent is due and my cable bill is due and my phone bill is due and my insurance is due and my water bill is due and my gas bill is due and my electricity bill is due and I have to get to my VA appointment, and I have to buy some dinners and there's just no way. No way I can let my goddamn car die before I'm through writing my notes.

AFTER a nap and a Swiffer and a brief hang-up on Helen's answering machine, I turned on the oven. I enjoy "Rooster" sandwiches, though without the tomato or lettuce that they always slop on at restaurants. Breaded chicken patties on a white hamburger bun, alongside cheese, a seep of mayonnaise, mustard and maybe ketchup, are mine. I realized as I sucked in the gas-blast that I was missing the season finale. I ran to the television while the oven hissed. Hit myself in the stomach, then below. It was already six minutes into the half-hour program! I ran back to turn off the gas, waved my hands around to chase the excess. Hit myself again. Bun crumbs on the linoleum had to be wiped. I turned the oven back on, pre-heated, positioned the patties on a nonstick tray, and slid it in.

At the climax of the program, the phone rang. I couldn't answer. Helen told the machine she was coming into town and wants to talk about how she screwed up both our lives and wants to change that and to please take a deep breath, and did I ever think about her suggestion that I adopt a cat? and . . .

I realized that I will be dead before she gets here, and more directly that these were my final finales. I pressed Volume Up on the remote.

The middles of the patties were uncooked, and strings of chicken slag lodged in my teeth. I ended up throwing most of the Rooster away, then waited for the commercials and rushed to the bathroom to vomit. As a child, I learned that you must flush the toilet to get low water before vomiting, to minimize backsplash.

CONVERSATIONS swirl from beyond my partition. None of them are about the first six minutes of the finale. The clerk with the dirty pants is slamming the door of the copy machine. I have got to get a two-day package together for Brendel's before the end of the day. I have got to finish my notes. I have got to finish my notes.

Darla

THE HIGH SCHOOL kids are out for summer, so all over this spit of a Mississippi town young women walk around in t-shirts over wet swimsuits. They cruise the Walgreens in coveys and type on thin phones, buy glamour mags and fla-vored water, their flip-flops slapping linoleum, their tan legs all over the place.

The boys in their wake call out Hey and Hey, y'all. They huddle up around hand-me-down trucks at the far end of the parking lot and trade licks. It's the worst.

YESTERDAY afternoon, Darla came home, pitched her keys on the counter and asked what was for dinner. My response was to ask what *she* wanted, because she vomits so much I can no longer guess what'll stay down.

"I don't know," she said.

"Taco Loco?" I said. "China Buffet?"

"No. But thanks for the healthy suggestions." She took a big breath and looked out the window. "Sorry," she said.

"Maybe I can go Taco Loco again. I just need to coat my stomach. God, it's burning up in here. Can we not turn on the air?"

"Sure, babe," I said. "Just tell me what you want."

"I don't know. Nothing," she said. "Just nothing."

"'Cause I'll eat whatever, Dar. I just don't have any money."

And so forth. Finally, she just took her pills with a glass of buttermilk. We then sat and watched Animal Planet beneath the hot draft of the ceiling fan. I thought about asking Darla why her boss had called the house again, looking for her during work hours. Thought about asking until reflux crept up my throat. But I stayed quiet. Since moving to Mississippi, I've come to mistrust confrontation; I am no longer sure where her wrong ends and my right begins.

During a scuba segment, Darla described the feeling of hatchling sea turtles crawling over your bare feet. "Flippers like flower petals," she said, her tone cottony and nostalgic. "Back in college, North Carolina, you'd go to the beach at night and shine a flashlight to guide them to the water. The light pollution, it—"

"You decide where you want to eat?" I cut in, not wanting any part of North Carolina, of Fort Bragg and that soldier she was with before me.

She didn't answer. At every commercial I'd ask again, and she'd say she didn't care. At some point I stood up from the couch, and went to grab a handful of quarters from the change-jar on my dresser. Darla could figure her own thing out; I was going to cash in for a set of two-for-one Walgreens pizzas.

I charged back through the den on my way out the door. "Since you can't tell me what you want to—"

She lunged up and ran to the bathroom to puke. This always makes me wonder if the pills even stick. I mean, what's the point?

An hour or so later, back on the couch, Darla said we didn't have that much romance left in us. In response I said, I love you, Dar, over and over, which was all I could think to say. I love you. But I love you. Gosh, I love you. How I love you. It felt like scooping water with a rake.

She was angry anyway. We were again watching television and she gave me positive news about her cell counts, and I only responded with, "That's great," at the commercial. But I love you. The cat had pulled out all kinds of tiny loops in the faded red upholstery. Darla had been skipping work but not coming home. How I love you. Nobody could stand to put the dishes in the dishwasher until everything piled up and stank and had gnats.

"Enough," I said a few minutes later. "Go get your suit on."

She turned the television volume up.

"Come on, get your swim trunks," I said. I held my gun finger to her head until I earned a smile. We no longer watched films. We no longer spoke of culture. Yet romance could still be rekindled by sneaking into the pool at High Cotton Apartments.

At the Quik Pik, I grabbed a twelve-pack, and Darla handed me the debit card, no problem. Things were looking up and we had plenty of gas in the car and she said she doesn't really mind my new little belly. We snuck into the complex pool and found nobody there, so I stripped my t-shirt off. She pushed me in and shrieked. There was a pool light at the shallow end but the light at the deep had gone out. Most of the water was opaque in contrast. The purple-green evening darkened into moonless black and the stars began to pop in stuttered levels of bright. At the edge of the patio fence, magnolia blossoms unfurled in ivory, and a dim yellow light cast down the coppery pebble inlay of the restroom wall. Darla swam to me and dipped her head back to get her hair out of her face, and for a moment we treaded the dark water and just looked at each other. She put her legs around me and we kissed as we sank, soft and slick and wet and lovely. I started to bob us off the bottom and move toward the light of the shallow end; up and down, up and down, I moved us towards that light. When the water level hit our chests, Darla told me she loved me. It felt like buckets. I wanted so badly to be with her, and knew she felt the same. But we hadn't brought any condoms, of course, so we just half smiled and looked past each other.

"What's that?" she asked. She disentangled from me, then swam to the shallow end and stood up. The water was illuminated and alien there, and a cluster of small, ghost-white objects rested on the bottom of the pool. There were eight or ten of them, bulleted in shape, undulating in the current from our movements.

"They're flower buds off of that magnolia," Darla said. "Sepals."

"No, babe," I said. "They're too white."

She stepped toward the blossoms, her waist rippling the water. She trapped one with her toes, reached under and pulled it up.

"Oh," she said, holding the object out to me. "It's a tampon. They're all just blanched-out, chlorinated tampons."

I looked around and saw that someone had thrown the sanitary receptacle from the ladies' room into a boxwood hedge by the lounge chairs. I guess they'd ripped it right off the wall, then dumped it out in the water as a joke.

High schoolers, I thought. Fucking high school vandals fucking up my everything.

THE Starbucks inside the Kroger sells the big paper from Jackson, and people leave sections lying around when heading off to work. Sometimes you pick up a Home and Garden, sometimes the Classifieds, or Religion. Sometimes those of us who *don't* head off to work pass the sections around and discuss. (Nobody ever talks about art or creative process, or the city, or the things Darla and I talked about when we lived *in* the city. No. That life got strangled out when we moved her back home.) All week long the Metro/State section has run installments about the last abortion clinic in the state. A group of lobbyists and politicians are trying to shut it down. From predawn to dusk that clinic is hemmed by evangels wagging posters of dead babies, alongside the Jackson PD and a PBS crew.

On my last day working at the Oriental rug shop over in Oxford, a leisure-class infant puked on the parquet floor. The mother then puppy-talked the baby while gauging a nineteenth century Persian Heriz. "Ow-noh," she said. "Awuh-woh." I refused to wipe up and was fired on the spot. Now Darla and I can't afford to blast the air-conditioning.

□   □   □

THE message Darla's boss left yesterday was no longer creepy genteel. It was not Wednesday's, *Just checkin' in on Darla to make sure she's feelin' okay.* Nor was it Thursday's, *Hey there, just sort of wantin' to know, well, where Darla might be. Give a call.* No. It was: *Darla, this is Jane Fisher. Call me the instant you get this.*

I rescued my first turtle a couple of months ago, right after I lost the rug store job. This was on a Saturday, and I remember the radio saying the temperature had hit ninety-four degrees by ten-fifteen a.m.—a record. I was coming back from dropping Darla off at Lu's, where they were going to have a Girl's Day Out in the country and drink Keystone Lite in Lu's aboveground pool. The open car windows baptized me in hot air as I gunned it over the straights of County Road 313. The old Mazda shuddered with every brake at the curves. I flew past mobile homes and wood-rot barns and dead cars in yards, and millions of tiny green cotton shanks in rows in the endless fields. Lu is a Gold Star, a wild-ass former professor whose Army reservist husband got KIA while deployed, not shot or bombed, but blown full of metal split rim and rubber after he forgot to cage a transport truck tire, then overinflated it. She retired on the Servicemembers' Group Life payout, and moved into a shotgun house in the sticks so she could rag economic segregation from beyond the academy. And make bonfires and drink beer.

Squares is what you call as-yet-fruitless cotton plants, Lu taught me. She likes Darla and me because we came to Mississippi from the city. Or, rather, Lu likes that Darla slung back home having put boots on the ground of the Great Cultural Beyond. ("You got more cred," Lu says, "than any dipshit Cultural Beyonder who judges the South from afar.") Lu gets drunk and weepy and calls her late husband Rubberneck, and tries to laugh, and wipes her eyes while she lights organic cigarettes. She claims to be pissed that he didn't leave her a decent combat story, a real whopper to throw around so folks could at least be impressed.

Anyway: It was a box turtle. I pulled over, and walked back to get it off the road. When I got close I realized its back end had been crimped by a tire. It hissed when I picked it up, and a chip of carapace plinked onto the asphalt. Its front legs clawed the air and its back legs flung on limp muscle. I paced around saying Jesus Christ a bunch of times while gingerly suspending the animal; there was tall dead grass on the edges of the fields and rusted wire fence, no water. A couple of old black men drove by in a green, early-seventies F-100, towing shoddy yard equipment on a deck trailer. They looked at me like I was wild. I was desperate to find some moisture in which to place the thing. "Please stop trying to kick your back legs," I begged. The shell was revealing itself to be a series of fractures. I figured the turtle would die but there was no way I could kill it. Finding no water, I carried it to a shady spot beneath a cluster of shortleaf pines. Huge black ants scurried atop the fallen needles beneath the trees.

"Sorry, man," I said, putting the turtle on the ground before walking away. "I promise I'm trying."

That night, while I was cleaning Darla's puke splats off the bottom of the boys' rim of the toilet, she got dropped off, drunk. She traipsed in and stood over me, and giggled at my yellow latex gloves.

"You never see these splats because of the way you piss," I said. "But they're here nonetheless." I then told her to hand me the Ajax.

TODAY, we were hauling ass on 278 East, west of Batesville, when I saw it. It was the biggest turtle I'd ever come across; a virtual extinction-in-waiting. Darla yelled when I whipped off the highway and into the manicured, pea-pebble drive of a restored plantation house. She couldn't believe I was stopping, as if things weren't bad enough.

We were supposed to be at the Sunflower Festival in Clarksdale, eating mounds of spicy crawdads with corn and sausage, sitting on the lawn near the main stage, listening to sacred steel music and drinking American beer. But halfway there we got in a fight so deep that both of us decided it best to turn the car around, drive right back out of the Delta, and drive beyond the hills, maybe all the way to Shiloh, where we'd walk in the knee-high grass of the battlefields and try to finally figure our shit out. Specifically, Darla confessed that she lost her job because she's been driving down to Jackson to loiter at the gates of the abortion clinic profiled in the news. She said she doesn't know why, or even what she thinks about it. Only that she's overwhelmed by the physical inability to pick a side.

One of the evangelicals she met is trying to forgive her her past sins. Darla has no idea how to respond to this, either.

Though the ass end of the Mazda wasn't really in the road, cars swerved and honked at us anyway. I got out and ran toward the massive turtle, which was parked at the centerline. Darla stayed in the car, in front of the antebellum plantation house, yelling obscenities.

The turtle was as big as a hubcap. When I picked it up it twisted its neck around to bite me, so I dropped it and darted back to the shoulder. Looking around, I noticed a small pool of gulley-wash at the edge of the cotton field behind me—a perfect refuge, if I could get it there without losing a finger.

I ran back to the car, told Darla to get the knife out of the glove box.

"I'm not saving or killing anything," she said.

"Come on, Dar."

"Why?"

"We can't just let the thing *die*."

The historic house we idled in front of was gorgeous: white column and portico and pediment, fanlight glass arching above the large doorway, and tall red cedars lining the long pebble drive. It sat comfortably back from the highway, its property defined by a thick, manicured hedge and tall iron gates. Acres of young, match-head cotton buds stretched out in rows over the adjacent fields. One lapse in drunken judgment less, one slip of latex more, and we both knew Darla would've lived in a place like this, without me.

She grabbed the knife. It was ninety-seven degrees. A passing semi concussed us in hot air.

"What do I do?" she asked, pinching the blade open. "Growing up, we never stopped for turtles."

"If it bites me, cut its head off."

"I won't," she said.

"You'll have to, or it'll never let go. I saw this on Animal Planet."

I jogged. She walked. Cars roared by, their draft air like slaps. Between them rose the scream of insects in the dry grass that fringed the fields. The snapper was still on the highway, intact but unmoving. I imagined the pavement was frying it inside its shell.

Darla caught up, and stared at the creature. "You sure?" she asked. "Behead it?"

"Hell, yes." I darted out and picked the turtle up just behind its middle, then held on tight as it hissed and snapped, and flailed its clawed feet. Darla marched beside me, holding the blade out as if she were going to thrust it into the turtle's neck whether she had to or not.

"Now, don't you feel good?" I asked when we made it back to the shoulder. I lifted the animal up, as if presenting a newborn. "Who knew that within a year we'd go from mass-transit nobodies to rural highway gods?"

Darla didn't even look, but just dropped the knife onto the ground. "I don't even get to know if I wanted one," she said, staring into the furrows, crying. "A kid, or even a stupid abortion. I don't even *get to know*, you know?"

"Darla, why are you— Why?" I was holding a snapping turtle on a highway outside of Batesville, Mississippi, in the swelter, trying to make the best of things. But Darla wouldn't let me. *She.* Because with Darla the fields are always a plague, the air a scorch over wasteland. All there ever is, is the over-and-again regurgitation of Darla, Darla, Darla; is how she's feeling at that instant, and how I'd better take good note; is the lust to remind her that she's a terrorist, to remind her that fucking her is like fucking a suicide vest; that fucking her is forever fucking some faceless furlough named fucking *Brent*, who was a hometown friend of her college roommate; who showed up in Wrightsville Beach after being out-processed from Bragg; who crashed their spring break condo with his combat stories and crippled manhood; who rolled Kite cigarettes and who was built like David and who was a stopwatch lay . . . and who planted in her the seed of a hard, unending cough; a cough which would manifest a few months later, long after he was gone, and long before I fell in love with her; a cough whose legacy is legions of vomit, alongside joint erosion and myalgia and associative vertigo, and red splotches on toilet porcelain and liver seizures and more vomit . . . and who came inside her, came inside. Got to come inside.

I turned from her and put the turtle down in the grass. Stared out into the expanse of cotton and listened to the bugs. Darla's belief that she would never again do better than me was bullshit. I hated that she would soon figure this out and leave.

"Anyway," she said, sniffled. "It's not just the light pollution, it's the moon."

"Dar, I'm sorry. I—"

"Those hatchlings in North Carolina? The moon's supposed to be their beacon to water, but the light pollution distracts. You take halogen flashlights and lead them right."

I watched the snapper claw through the dry grass, then dive beneath the brown water in the gully. I knelt down and picked up a twig, and poked at the pebbles and bits of safety glass on the shoulder. A minute later, Darla wiped her nose with the heel of her hand, then mouthed the words, Let's go.

So Bored in Nashville

BARS AND BOOZE and lacquer and glass and smoke and teevee and tourists and shots, and pit-stop at Randall's to chop up a Xanax, to snort then smoke then back to the bars. In this city, through the bars, we wind up packed in a room full of ads. Living ads, that is, sexy and skimpy young women ads. New England or Oklahoma transplants, wannabe country stars clad in fishnets and bra tops, hot pants and logos, and who proffer shots of some dye-injected Extreme Liquor product. A temp job, they swear, they serve you straight out of their mouths, out of their navels, wherever, no problem. For ten bucks a pop they make ten bucks an hour, while your lips suckle shots off of their amazing young stomachs. And they're dying to sing, will do anything to demo. (All of this action in a Vandy sports bar, not an airport strip club, let alone a music industry hang.) And tomorrow I leave, for Forts Jackson then Benning. Signed the contract when the Army offered me 11B, Option 4: Airborne Infantry. I am twenty-six and terrified. Yet I felt compelled to follow through after the recruiters told me how difficult it was to secure this assignment. How rare it is these days to earn Option 4, Airborne, war on and all.

Hoo-ah! they barked. You tha man, man!

Randall and I depart that bar, we drive on. He says zero about my deployment. We pay cover, we squeeze into an East Nashville venue, find another Brooklynesque band, another huddle of white hipsters in white V-neck t-shirts whose everything is constructed by camouflaging their incomes, by folding tattooed arms across their chests, and/or nodding and/or spying at their phones. Superb denim, everywhere. We drive off. Drop twenty bucks to park on bustling and hyper-sold Second Avenue: Hard Rock Café, Coyote Ugly, chain, chain, etc., etc. At a pseudo-upscale music hall, stuffed with pseudo-upscale music industry fakes, reclaimed wood and iron, taxidermy mounts, Randall yanks me into a hallway and flask-feeds me bourbon. Tells me he can't get away from unknowns who want to write songs with him—Hey, man, let's write; Hey, Randall, let's write—everywhere he goes, because they know that their chances of landing their first album cut are stronger with his name on as cowriter. (A couple years back, Randall wrote a chestnut called "Urban Cowgirl," a one-off departure from his nonpaying folk songs. After the song was cut by a cosmetic cowboy, it topped the Top 40, and made Randall a universe of cash. Now nobody artsy and literate and frustrated will hang out with him. He is and forever will be the "Urban Cowgirl" sellout.) Randall hates this process, this creative suck-off, yet he does the same thing to more established songwriters: calls them to cowrite, wedges into their conversations at industry gatherings, at industry bars, pumping gossip like heartbeats, desperate to book a session, to redefine himself. I do not call him out on this. We are all chasing better narratives. Besides, truth is, I only want to be called out by *him*. I am desperate for his protest, or his permission to deploy. Because Randall and I have been each other's go-to forever, over a thousand nights of dive bar and misquoted verse and booze-drenched guitar pull . . . and through his mother's distal dystrophy, and the guilt he had over avoiding her, her withered, alien forearms and brittle legs . . . and through the time we dragged his PA onto his back porch the instant the sun tickled the frozen January horizon, cranked J. J. Cale while slugging a bottle of Pappy, then woke up as two of Nashville's Finest draped us in Mylar emergency blankets, and . . . yet he does not seem to care about my military aptitude score, or the fallout with my job, or about what happened with *her*, how she never even called me back to tell me goodbye, or about my need to prove to her and my dad and my boss and everyone that I am worth something. That I am a Man from the South. Every time I try to prod Randall about this he says nothing. I'd been waiting on Option 4, Airborne, and I didn't think the recruiters would call back, and in fact had come to think of my whole visit to the recruiting office as a big, reactive joke to her having left me. A counterpunch to her giving up on us. But three months later they did call back. They said, Okay, you've got it, Airborne, grunt, and then barked and all, Hoo-ah, on the phone, it was so fakey this bark. It was another gray morning, a hungover Tuesday all email all phone all filing and process. Fakey bark fakey office fakey music fakey everything, and so I called her and got sent to voice mail, and I left a message telling her I what I was about to do, all but daring her to call me and talk me out of it. And the morning burned off and I heard nothing from her: no phone or text no email no nothing. So I drove to the recruiter's office on my lunch break, and signed the six-year contract; I took his high five and then went and got drunk. And tomorrow I'm off, Forts Jackson then Benning, 11B, Option 4, No bitches allowed in Airborne, Hoo-ah! they said. So fakey, I know, but what else is there to do but follow history? Men go to war to be men worth a damn. Their statues and movies are everywhere, forever.

I can't stop checking my phone.

On the tourist-littered sidewalk we banter with drunk, middle-aged couples, feeding them elaborate lies about the deaths and trysts of country music stars "on this very *f*-in' spot, y'all." I am terrified we will never do this again. And the back of every blond head in this town is hers, and love is a veggie skin scraper-offer. And flat-screen televisions deliver the sports news above us, in every bar corner, muted. And sports and death and brass and wood and pool balls crack, glasses fall to shatter. We drive, we drive, we drink, we drive, we zip past ads on coasters, ads in stalls, ads on walls on TV on streets on girls on cab roofs on radio on billboards on stadiums. We slap down the plastic for two more shots, a toast of Bud Light and American Spirit as sidekick while we post up and play Spot the Black Guy. Because rarely in this growth-industry city, in these bars of brick-and-barn-wood, and fusiony kitchens and midtown art studios and progressive, boutique, bottle-tree enclaves are there ever any real live Black Guys to know—though the majority of new urbanites spew their love of diversity. (I have no BFs but I swear I would if they were around here; my recruiter was African-American, ex-DB at UT.) Neither of us scores a point. And Randall talks to smiling belles in designer clothes; he flirts but then falters when they determine he's not from the South, that he doesn't have the requisite pedigree to match his requisite money. We curse this predetermination as we storm out the door, into the car, stabbing farther into the city, and do not talk about me. Cops block the arteries, so we cut through the alleys, past cats darting and tourists pissing in shadow, chain link binding the job sites beside us, massive wounds of rebar and churned mud and crane and more crane, and we're sweat-soaked so thirsty as we hit the touristy honky-tonks of Lower Broadway, where tourists in new denim call for Top 40 Country, earning scowls from the finely tuned rockabilly yips who still pilgrim downtown for a swing on the dance floor. The den so drunken, the burgers spit on the grill. Telecaster, Telecaster, the registers rattle credit slips while two-steppers slip on beer-splattered linoleum.

Closing time, hoo-ah! I looked everywhere but did not see her. These had been *our* bars and *our* closing times and always *our* last dances. Our drunken public make-outs and slurred-word squabbles. I wanted so bad just to tell her that tonight was the last night. To see her face when I told her I was GONE after this, I mean GONE. Surely, that would bump the needle. Make her miss me just a little bit.

Surely, for sure I would matter to her again.

We drive on. Randall works the radio while I think through an encyclopedia of the ways I would tell her; she always begs me, *No, don't go.* Last Call behind us, we race to the convenience store, get there in the nick for a battery of 40-ounce bottles. Our redneck clerk is clad in a red-white-and-blue-blaring Tennessee Titans jersey. He watches a tummy-tuck teevee show, locks the door behind us and bids us, Be careful, y'all. And on to the drive-thru, to millions of tiny, steamed sliders, to mini chili dogs, all bite-sized but with biggie fry, as served by a navy-blue-vest-wearing, middle-aged Latina. Her first-generation accent and bright blond streaks, and wonderful smile. Her front teeth edged in dull gold, she is plump and headsetted and a goddamn late-night nobody for seven-two-five an hour, and whom Randall laughs at, so pissy drunk he is, throwing his request of, "More . . . uh . . . ketchup, por fay-vor," hee hee, before skidding off, before he and I inhale malt liquor while carving the one-way downtown streets, back, forth, back, forth, side street to side, silent save for the sound of hot wind through cracked windows, the sound of the car lighter popping, the sound of our latching like babies to gold lager bottles until, somehow, at last, amazingly, we end up atop the tallest downtown hill. Randall cuts the motor and we get out and wobble, clutching food bags and 40s at the foot of the white, ionic columns of the massive Tennessee State Capitol, Greek Revival, 1859, judging our fair southern town from on high. Who knew we had such unguarded access to this place? Where do these people get off feeling safe?

"Man, look at that," Randall slurs.

A gasping view of nude America, asleep and dreaming. So quiet, so pure. Ad-free and lovely, sexless and serene. Our capitol is skirted by fine landscape architecture. By granite and bronze memorial. By a sweeping, grassy mall that flows downhill like an emerald gown-train, stitched at the periphery by bulbs of antique lamplight. The space honors President Polk (Congress at age twenty-nine), Sergeant Alvin York

(Medal of Honor at thirty-one), Sam Davis, Boy Hero of the Confederacy (martyred at twenty-one). All represented in statue, all soundtracked by third-shifters in beater cars whose hanger-hung mufflers reverberate up and around the massive statehouse. Every single bit of this place is a remembrance to, or declaration of, cataclysm. To wins and losses by warrior men—with a nod of course to the Women of the Confederacy Monument.

We stand atop a hill of government and history, gorging on McShit and drinking our 40s. And Randall asks, What the hell, man? when I shoot snot on the historic marker, and take a piss on the presidential tomb. He curses when I smear ketchup and cow meat on the Senate door handles, then fling pickles on the fanlight windows.

"Andrew Jack-son, Indian slaughterer." I prance about, singing in schoolyard melody about Nashville's favorite son. Mustard and chili will slick up this cultural lineage; that state flag's coming down now for an ass-wipe. *"Thom-as Jefferson, slave-whipping hypocrite,"* is my motto of centralized government. I sling trash like confetti; stacks of wadded wax paper and bags, napkins and condiment packets tumble in the breeze over the expansive green lawn. Wish to God I could spray a shit on the stars. *"Jeffer-son Da-vis, captured in a dress by the Yan-kee grunts—hoo-ah!"* I cry. Smash my bottle on the bronze of Jackson on mount, then slash at the fetlocks in hopes he'll spill like Saddam.

"Enough!" Randall marches over, grabs my arm and shakes me. "Enough."

I pull free and get in his face. "Defend this!"

"Nothing to defend. I just don't want to go to jail, man."

"Please," I beg. "I've signed the contract, I am going to war. So tell me you need these people, this place. This memory. Tell me that you can't live without us."

He jiggles his keys in his pocket and turns from me. "Love you, pal," he says. "All I am is sad. Real sad."

We depart.

Chicks

I DRIVE BACK into the beige haze of the Valley. Waste away on the weak side of hot. "Smog Index must be ten," I mumble to myself, in bumper-to-bumper traffic, my body longing to sweat. I don't know for sure if indices or numbers are used to calculate smog. I *believe* someone told me that when the L.A. horizon starts to spoil, its tint reminiscent of a dirty aquarium, a Smog Index or Alert is issued, the authorities instructing us to seal up in residence, to breathe only conditioned air.

Smog doesn't matter, anyway. What matters is that I've forgotten whether this someone was a Someone I should remember to remember: man, woman, curious, queer, producer, director, dealer, what? What matters is that I shove on the wall of an industry which mandates that I not only know Everyone, but know exactly what they've got going on, when they're hot, what they're hot for, and most importantly what I can do to make them hot for me.

It is seventy-nine degrees in Southern California, again.

Sunlight spears past the cream vinyl visors as I turn onto Ventura Boulevard. The silver pocket watch in the car's center console keeps erratic time. Dry breeze through the open windows fans the script pages on the passenger's seat.

Breeze or not, these pages aren't going anywhere. Not today. Apparently, my writing remains stuck in bassackwards South Carolina. It seems I don't have a grasp on the language or thoughts or physiology of real-world chicks. Chicks, chicks, chicks.

THIS was part of my pitch to the Producer, earlier today: "Ultimately, the story is an old-school romance in which the innocence of a kiss is infinitely more valuable and, well, more *noble* than sex."

He sighed.

"If you will, follow me, here," I continued. "People are overpumped with sex. Movies, television, commercials, ads, books, e-books, pop-ups, wherever. What they forget about, what they lack, is honesty. Sincerity. Tenderness. So they'll devour this story. A young couple, desperate in love—only he's shipping off to war. We follow their last night together, until they part at daybreak on the fragility of a kiss."

"Sure, kid," he said, his words a dollop of disinterest. "Hey? I get it. And the war thing sells like crack. But here's the problem. You can't base a major motion-picture budget on some sappy kiss. On a fragile whatever. Mature audiences need more—even from a chick flick. They *crave* more. Hey? Know what I think?"

"What's that?" I said, I say, again and again, in meeting after meeting, in squat stucco buildings augmented by outrageous European cars, by jasmine vines that struggle up pink walls with ornamental wooden doors.

He noted something clever. His pristine teeth screamed monthly scrape; the flawless skin of his cheeks, abrasion. And as it all came together, teeth and scrape and stucco, my disappointment dragged me to yet another memory of yet another faceless L.A. Moment. To the words of yet another ghost. This Someone—whomever they were—made the observation that Los Angeles architecture is either (A) holding firm to the 1970s, or (B) represents the far evolution of sexless capitalism: Strip Mall, City of the Future. Either way, this city is a fundamental counter-aesthetic to the dignified militarism of home. Where is the memorial? The genteel remembrance of strife?

"Ammo or AOC?" the Producer asked, his finger poised to press on this black desktop orb.

"Sorry?"

"Never apologize, kid. What do you think? Ammo or AOC? I'm meeting a client later."

"Trick answer," I answered. "The patio at AOC—only, before it was AOC. When it was still Orso. Anyway, I'll never understand why anyone goes beyond the Chateau. Cliché or Q-score be damned. You just can't kill the hang."

The amount of time I spend memorizing industry blogs is nauseating.

"Good," he said. He put his fingertip on the orb and instructed, "Set up drinks at Bar Marmont. And put a hold on Room 64, in case things turn fun."

□   □   □

IF you frame the narrative correctly, the $10 bill in my wallet is exponentially powerful. A potential game-changer. Ten bucks equals three gallons of unleaded gas. Therefore, worst-case scenario, in stop-and-go traffic, it equals sixty-six miles. Sixty-six miles equals four round trips over Laurel Canyon. Four trips over Laurel Canyon are potentially four pitch meetings, out of which I only need one to pop. Statistically speaking, this could be the last time I have to worry about . . .

Who am I kidding? Make that one gallon and a $7 pack of Winstons. Make it twenty-two miles and sixteen waking hours of nicotine, alongside the heartbreak of having to list another Bolex lens on eBay, in order to make rent and buy *Variety*. As complement, go ahead and make it be the scream of a failed CV axle joint, or the driver's-side window whose crank handle snapped off, meaning that you must roll the thing up using pliers, every time you park in this city of thieves.

The white plastic bag on the passenger's seat floor contains Ralph's eponymous organic spinach, Ralph's eponymous frozen pizzas, and a six-pack of cold, cheap American pilsner. (Ralph's grocery does not yet offer generic beer.) Got $10 cash back, which I had to ask for special, since the lowest option on the checkout screen was $20.

YOU know those glass electricity globes? Those electricity-filled glass globes in kids' museums that generate multicolored lightning? She was like that. Her spark was wit and literariness and sentimentality, and a tiny white dog-bite scar that curled off her upper lip like a bass clef. She had a penchant for spouting high-minded conspiracy theory, e.g., Kafka Predicted the Holocaust. A disdain for the paper-white lily, for banana nut bread from a package, e.g., Martha White (though if one must buy premixed banana nut bread, she figured one might as well go with Martha White). All sorts of details. And, point being, if she was that globe, and if you touched the globe softly, the lightning softly struck back. If you placed hands fully on it, it crackled and thrust in kind. Leave it alone and it, she, did her thing in beautiful solitude.

I left South Carolina six weeks after our first date, having already quit my job and sold my everything to move west and sell a story.

"Superb timing," she said, then gave me the antique pocket watch as a parting gift.

I sit out here and hock my narrative and make her be the balance. At a stoplight, under the smog-fed palms, she is always the balance I'm missing.

SUBPLOT: I can't believe there aren't automatic car washes at the filling stations in this town. In the seven months separating the South from Southern California I haven't seen one. Not *one*, among the endless pimples of gas pumps. And everyone here loves cars like money and breathing smog and driving slowly, stuttering through the near-dead breeze, primping in the Prozacian semi-heat, banging their monotonous remixes at you. And the cars are always beautiful, and certainly more important than the squat buildings that define the majority of Southern California. And despite the whole "green" thing, most of the cars still run on fuel. And they *do* make gas stations with attached car washes, elsewhere in the United States. My father owned one, and growing up I worked there every summer, and by worked there I mean I learned how to work. Yet here in Los Angeles, no.

"POINT being, you've gotta think like a modern chick," the Producer said, his lips launching a fleck of spittle. He then fumbled with a crystal paperweight worth more than my car. "Hey? The war thing is money right now. And your dialogue, themes and stakes are good. But they're dated, kid. This is yesteryear shit—only not in the period-piece sense." He checked his watch.

"But," I said.

"But women are more *human* than that, you know? Women *want*. They're empowered and sexy and smart, and, hey? They've sure got us by the balls, right?"

This isn't an important film. Not a period piece or art film. Not even a chick flick, really. It's a romantic heart-tugger written to attract hyper-consumer, disposable-income teen girls. It's as dense as popcorn, maybe lighter. A squishy wartime anecdote. Looking at the Producer I wanted to scream that he was missing it all. Adulterating the fantasy, sodomizing innocence. Yet because I am so tired of this exchange, so tired of how these things starve out, I just said, "Yeah, by the balls. I'm with you, and I'll revisit immediately. Rewrite's not a problem. In terms of basic plot, though, I think I can still keep the kiss, only add—"

He stabbed his finger into the black orb. "Marcy? Marcy, hop down here for a sec, will ya?"

SUBPLOT: Though *vital* is defined as time inside the stucco offices of Hollywood or Beverly Hills, *affordable* is Roscoe crossing Sepulveda, in the Valley. It is a confederacy of low-rider VW Beetles and drag-modified Japanese cars. It is bilingual title loans and barred windows, and windowless bars whose daytime clientele loiter in the parking lots, smoking joints, their backs against the pastel-colored beaches of mural-covered walls.

On the street in front of my rented duplex, near Roscoe and Sepulveda, statuesque black boys swagger by after school, their white uniform shirts slung over their bare, muscled shoulders. Among other glories, there is brilliance in the way they launch a seamless "fuck you" or "bitch ass" bark into the meter of their conversation, precisely as they pass me by, in order to showcase aggression, to let me know who owns the space.

At Roscoe and Sepulveda exist endless chop shops and immigration consultant offices and Kountry Kitchen restaurants and titty bars and grit on the curb, and sublime Mexican food and hot, dry heat, radiated by street signs and strip malls and gas stations with no car washes.

□   □   □

MARCY, in a black Italian suit, was quite sexy in that vague, TV way. She bit the side of her thick bottom lip and gave this snappy introduction that I will no doubt remember later, wondering where, amid the blur of boy sluts and beggars, poseur glamour and chrome, I heard it. The Producer provided her a six-second coverage of my entire story, before asking, "So you tell me, Marse. As a woman, are you satisfied by a flimsy kissing bout?"

In the notch between his question and her answer I thought of my pocket watch. Imagining the cadence of its second hand conjured my grandmother's yawning drawl. In memory, she told me, again, the story of she and my Poppum's first hours of love, just before he shipped for Europe, and later the Pacific theater. "We's just a sliver past twenty," G-ma said, noting the fitted grasp of their palms, "like a rhyme." She told me that the night before he deployed, the Carolina moon shot through the trees, and lit up the ground in a jigsaw of leaf shadow. Unable to afford a phonograph, she said they waltzed to the croon of cicada, to slow, sidereal measure, the July humidity held at bay by the salty coastline breeze.

My grandparents, as their forebears had been, and as their children would be, were created by pending and consequent separation. They were sprung from a chasm generated by conflict. By man by woman by war—the end. There can be no other southern narrative.

As Marcy spoke I could almost feel the sublime, sticky heat

of home: How it slicks your body, driving you to the honest edge of tolerance. How it begs you to dive down, beneath the cold convicted waters of the dead green Atlantic. True heat is at least substantial and wet, at least passionate.

"Osculation," Marcy said, pulling me back. "I understand where you're trying to go. The whole, like, woman-on-a-pedestal vibe? But listen to me—now. And remember this if you remember nothing else: that's *chauvinism*, man, not chivalry. Period." She stared at me for impact, then continued. "In reality? From the standpoint of both woman and viewer? After two acts loaded with the thrust of a countdown romance, I'd better be getting the love fucked out of me."

My dear god, I wanted to fuck the love *into* her the instant her rose lips rested—but just as quickly realized my selfishness, and once more reiterated my opinion. My code.

That's the fundamental difference out here. They have simply forgotten the past.

I drag to a stop at the multi-pumps outside a Gas-N-Save, prepared to part with this new, last ten bucks. The script falls quiet. The reflection of the watch hits the windshield. Pizza thaws, beer drips. A clutter of loitering little *vatos* in wife-beater T's prop up on the far end of the store wall, burning cigs mixed with weed, their chests bowed out.

I walk over to prepay but freeze up when an enormous gold 1970-something Cadillac convertible squeals onto the lot. The velocity and violence feel like an ambush.

◻   ◻   ◻

"HEY? Look, kid," the Producer said. "Normally, I'd thank you and tell you I'd be in touch—and basically flush you out of this office, with more concern for my freakin' ficus tree. But I like you. Really do. Your style's strong and you've got germs of good ideas. So, hey? Let me impart some key advice. Get a grip on your audience. Translate your talent into something more modern."

He excused himself briefly. Touched the black orb, and he commanded (to an assistant? to Marcy?), "On second thought, put a hold on the Argyle. Fuck the fusty Chateau."

He kept calling me kid. He's my age. Went to college with my cousin.

"What was I . . . ?" he asked. "Oh, yeah. Hey? I know what you're thinking: *This asshole's asking me to sell out.*"

"No," I said. "I wasn't."

"Yeah, I know. The big bad *sellout* of your ideals. Christ, how often do I hear it? I'll tell you how often. Every day, all day."

"Really, I wasn't—"

"But listen. *You're not selling out if you cater to what people want.* Are you? Are you selling out if you're sharing real emotions with a real audience?"

How can this be? I'm sold. So sold. Oversold. I couldn't possibly sell more on this thing.

IF.

If you met someone who chose to live of, but beyond, the façade of dogwood-flowered, South Battery coastline; of, but beyond, the high-heel click on terra-cotta patio and lime-rind-and-seersucker; if she chose to move beyond historic district fund-raising and neo-southern cuisine . . . and who instead sought out the cracked concrete back porch of a Gullah-owned shrimp shack; who found inspiration in a shrimp burger with a side of under-the-table, Styrofoam-cupped American beer—would you leave her?

Could you? If she knew how to overthrow the manicured ritual of a Kiawah Island wedding weekend, where paunchy young men in Brooks Brothers knits drain designer beers at every emerald putting green, while their counterpart women, women whose southern lips have grown thin from years of décor-smiling, sit bunched up in air-conditioned villas, sipping premix mojitos? If. If she could be *of* this culture, yet scoff it all off for a midnight drunken joyride over marsh road? If her brown hair flew out the window, fanlike, as the two of you traded hard opinions of Paris '68, of F. Scott v. Hemingway, or for that matter of the Only Ernest that Really Matters Anyway—Ernest Tubb? If your collective ceremonial garb was balled up on the backseat; if you had nine bucks between you for beer, gas and adventure? If you wound up chilly and huddled together on the predawn beach, wrapped up in a cocoon of musty, wedding-band quilt?

Could you leave her? And if you could, how on earth would you get over it?

GAS-N-SAVE is out of Winstons, so I buy a pack of generics. Give up the ten bucks and get the balance in fuel. I scan the door-side magazine rack while the clerk rings me up. The cover of a woman's journal pimps a vibrant nineteen-year-old actress whose name we all know. Her pout and airbrushed flesh support the headlines "Sex Quiz: Rate Your Mate" and "Seductive Lingerie for Bedroom-Bound Babes." I wonder if I need to start reading these things, to grow.

At the pump adjacent my car a young *pachuco* and his girlfriend—the passengers of the golden Cadillac convertible—yell at each other. He is wiry and postured, wearing baggy khakis, black kung-fu slippers and a white muscle shirt. Not American, perhaps not even a man; I look at him and critique this stereotype, as if he's been snatched off the street by Production.

She, however, is radiant and original. Uncommonly tall. The sun is sheeny in her cascading black hair. Her skin color is somewhere between chocolate and butter, and I imagine her of royal lineage (Oaxacan being the only identifier I am familiar with). The syllables her wine-colored lips splay, the intermittent "fuck you's" and "bastard's," as churned within glorious Spanish, crescendo over him with feminine mastery.

"HEY?" the Producer asked. "I mean, really, kid, why do you create?"

"Who knows anymore?" I replied.

"To *connect*, right? Right?"

"Yeah, sure." I'd had enough. By that point I no longer bore an awareness of anything, save the platinum letter opener he used to pick at his fingernails. And the fact that I wished Marcy would come back.

"'*Yeah, sure*,'" he mocked me. "That's what all you cred-heads say: '*I write in order to connect with people*,' or '*Because I want to share in our universal human emotion*,' or some other humble horseshit. But, hey? Interview over, these darlings don't really care about the Everyman. They're too intellectual, too precious with their 'art.'" He paused for effect, then pointed at me. "Now, THAT, kid, is selling out."

"I'm listening to you. Now you listen to me. This script is—"

"Quit trying to be high-minded and slick. Focus on telling a *story*."

THE pending violence between the Mexican couple is too real. I dive into myopic action: remove the hose from the pump, select the gas grade, unlock the gas cap, insert the spout. Remember a pitch I overheard, somewhere, about a band of Communists in the twenties who stormed the offices of the *Los Angeles Times*, slaughtering everyone on site. I think of the unassailable truth locked inside Marcy. Beneath the saline monuments in her chest she knew the idealism I was pitching, and she knew it wasn't some elitist avoidance of sex or combat. Because I do know chicks. I do I do I do.

Maricón! Puto! You're no man, you limp pendejo motherfucker.

I don't dare look at them. Rather, I force myself deeper into memory as the gas fumes embalm me. I fix my eyes on the pocket watch, and inhale, and daydream.

At my going-away party, she said, "Don't get all Los Angeles on us."

"Impossible," I replied. "You exist, here. So I'll never really leave."

Malapalacas con grapacomundos y fucking stupid cohbomayaca!

There, on the edge of the party guests, she hovers. She sparks and crackles and is a thousand times warmer than the California sun, but without a whisper of its dry suffocation.

Órale, *homies*, the Mexican woman says to the young *vatos*, and starts mocking her man. *Look at the* cabrón *who thinks he can handle a real Chicana. Thinks he can—*

The *pachuco* slaps the woman in the jaw, and I am right back in the Valley. Full of fire and love and bad timing and southern manhood, I have a good idea about what to do now. I know exactly what to do now.

He flicks his cigarette into her black hair, calls her a whore.

"Hey?" I shout at him. "Get away from her, man."

Like a gunshot he's on me, the first blow knocking stars into my vision. He strikes and smashes until I fall, the grated parking lot ripping my chin. He then mocks my accent while kicking my ribs—*Get-uh-way frum her may-un!* The *vatos* cut up in the background.

A kick to the head launches me beyond the liminal; I am home now, with her. I savor her electricity, respire her scent. Tangled up in a patchwork quilt, we watch the daybreak lighten the black-green Atlantic. We kiss, forever, beneath the dry rustle of palmetto leaves. Then I leave her. True story.

Ferric saliva, alongside a "Hurry the fuck up, girl!" drag me back to Southern Cal. My ribs hurt so bad that I shiver. I try to stand up but my knees buckle, so I just kneel on the oil-stained concrete. Wipe the blood from my mouth, spit.

I look up to see the Latina steal the last of my possessions from the car. She runs to join her partner in the golden convertible. They look at me and burst into laughter.

"Later, bitch!" the woman yells at me, then kisses her man deeply. As the car peels out, she slings my pizza like a Wham-O. When the Cadillac meets the street, she hurls my script in the air. A litter of loose pages arch and flit in the couple's wake, tumbling high against the backdrop of endless L.A. strip mall.

Blending into the streetscape, highlighted by chrome and asphalt, I know this Mexican woman is no criminal. Rather, she is lovely, ethereal. Primed with personal agency. She steals my pocket watch and conspires to humiliate me, yet I can't help but smile, and picture her a shade away from rediscovering some innocence, deep, deep inside.

Because I know about chicks.

Clean

THROUGH THE BATHROOM door I thanked Joy very much for her critique, and then stepped into the shower, which was scalding. No response came. I tucked my left arm behind my back, clasped my right wrist, and clenched. Forced myself to endure the temperature while staring down her beloved loofah. (This was all, of course, following shave and defecation, both of which had been peppered by Joy's grooming suggestions.) Yes, I got in, tucked and clasped as always, and began to boil myself. After some minutes, my body vibrating like a tuning fork, no fistula for release, the water at last became sufferable, at which point I exhaled, clutched the bar soap, and began to clean.

There had been no showers in the desert for weeks at a stretch. There had been bitch baths in the tent, by flashlight. The sand scoured the folds of your body, was gritty in your waistline and nostrils, anus and lungs. Here, my white briefs were folded into thirds, and placed atop the cool closed lid of the commode. My towel and talc were at the ready.

At some point I was redeployed. Given back to lower

Alabama, to the blanket of wet heat, the punctuation of air-conditioning. I then spent years in school because I couldn't determine anything else with traction. Money is such a limp conquest. Bitch baths are when you wipe yourself clean with a rag. Joy was the girl who had sent letters of dull optimism while I was at war: tiny circles dotted her *i*'s; she promised to meet me on the base tarmac when I returned, etc. The loofah was a queer little bundle of lime-colored plastic netting, dangling by a soft rope from this hook on a suction cup. She bought it at a bath store in an outlet mall off I-10, and I made fun of it. And her.

And the university offered me a part-time thing immediately after graduation. Male department bigwigs asked me about the war during the interview, and I said only that I didn't know what to say, and they nodded back at me and were silent, as if I were withholding something magical. Yes, they offered me this adjunct teaching thing, alongside this other job thing, where I show up at alumni fund-raisers and talk to rich or important men, my hands constantly scooping peanuts. Or rather, I *don't* talk while the men nod and reflect on me and on war. I eat peanuts, peanuts.

Bo-ring, Joy says, her index finger like a pistol at her temple.

I stood beneath the piping-hot water and thought of these men, their nose hairs protruding like spider legs, their theoretical empathies and deconstructionist blurbs, and something clicked: though I was already clean, I decided to grab hold of that loofah, douse it in her verbena body wash, then lather myself.

It felt good and slick and yet grainy, explosive. Shhh, I

thought. I hated that Joy was right, shhh. I then thought of the gay cowboy movie she recently made me watch, and wondered whether or not I had, would, or was turning homosexual. To counter this I started to hum to mumble to sing the lyrics to an old song by the Stone Temple Pilots, the one whose guitar riff sounds like a rape, before finally stumbling into thoughts on yesterday's *Ellen*, which featured a southern trust-funder who made a documentary about being rich. He wanted to be not-rich, like, culturally, but without having to lose his actual money. He confronted his rich father about this with a video camera. *I am a man, a man*, the song says, maybe. *I know you want what's on my mind*. I was so alone in that shower. The verbena reminded me of a Faulkner novel.

When your unit is preparing to redeploy home you have to use power washers to cleanse every single speck of Holy Land from all equipment: tanks, Humvees, tents, etc. Every goddamn speck, they order, as you stand there, your sweat evaporating before it even has a chance to lick the skin, the water pressure so intense it peels paint; so intense that when it touches you, when it barely glances the inside crook of your elbow, it gives you a third-degree burn. Happens so fast that it doesn't even hurt—and then the skin is gone, and it does hurt, big time. Anyway, given all the other tasks you've had to swallow, cleaning sand off of armored personnel carriers seems anticlimactic, fucking stupid.

I brushed the loofah across my abdomen and thought briefly of my embarrassingly small TIAA-CREF retirement portfolio, and then of this quirky kid, Alex, who makes semi-decent grades in my Contemporary Issues class. He's a frat boy, wealthy and light-brown-headed, with those madras shorts that all southern boys sport. I pictured his soft, swoopy bangs, and again worried that I might be homosexual, and looked down at my penis as the water spouted off the end. It did not stretch forth. I then worried that maybe my penis wasn't stretching forth because of the severed ear that Alex brought into my office hours—but not because I wasn't homosexual for him. I then decided to purposely think *about* the gay cowboy movie, and, conversely, about Joy fellating me, up and down, in tandem with her hand, and how fond I can be of this. There was no response to either. There was a ton of foam in the loofah net, in proportion to the small amount of verbena soap employed.

Joy says that peanuts are the good kind of fat. The problem is that a can of nuts lists 39 Pieces as a Serving—but no mention of whether or not these pieces are whole peanuts or half, both of which populate every peanut container and bowl. The southern trust-funder-turned-documentary-filmmaker was one of many über-wealthy heirs who appeared on *Ellen* to talk about how they could distance—and had distanced—themselves from their fortunes, to induce social change. In the desert, there was this American Indian cook, Choctaw so he said, around sixty, who was a fevered alcoholic and who brewed applejack wine and took his bitch baths out of the same industrial-sized pot he cooked chow with. Somebody saw him doing so one night and word of "sick-ass Indian water" streaked through camp. People switched back to dehydrated MREs for a day or two, and cursed his filthy breed, then showed back up for pasta with fake butter and garlic powder anyway. It was just too good for racism or body oils.

When you think about it, contemporary issues aren't that contemporary—Alex the frat boy said in class. I mean, like, what the hell is Vietnam, anyway? he asked. Are we not *so* over that?

Social change. Well, to tell you the truth, I would rather have fought alongside faggots than women, because the lust for women makes straight male soldiers not pay attention, and maybe not pay attention to not getting themselves killed—I said to Joy, at which point she didn't speak to me until I explained that this view did not preclude women from being top-notch killers. Only that straight men were sex pigs who shouldn't be distracted in a combat zone. None of the university presses wish to consider my scholarship. Joy tells me to perhaps consider some other career, something that pays. Says that I'm a veteran and a man and white, so how hard can it be? I worry that I will deposit remainder feces on the loofah, but I must scrub effectively. People were hooking up all over the desert. Male and female soldiers could overlook the rankest of places, the most stable of marriages, just to get it on for a few hot seconds. The thing is, we had to fuck so much because we just weren't shooting enough people to change things, to wash away the fear.

Alex came to my office hours two days after we watched a documentary film about 1960s Birmingham and those black girls who got bombed at church. He was strangely giddy, lugging a full backpack. He came in and looked around and said: I know this is, um, weird, but . . . and then pulled out a mason jar filled with dark pink liquid and a bobbing ear. Thousands of tiny floaties swirled in the brine. He told me he found it in his great-aunt's basement after she died. He, Alex, tries to trash-talk anything or anyone deviant in contemporary issues. I'm certain this is because he is homo, and afraid.

Indeed, in tandem with the loofah device, a minuscule amount of verbena body wash is enough for the entire process: right armpit, then across chest into left armpit, back to chest, down to penis, anus, legs, anus again, pubic hair, legs and anus and rinse and inspect and rinse. This is enough. My back stays under the hot water, and I imagine it lobster-colored. So damn hot I sometimes wonder if afterwards I could take a dry towel and rub enough friction up to remove the flesh. I know that I am not attracted to Ellen's turncoat heir. I take hold of my penis again and flip-flop it up and down in a nice rhythm while thinking of his segment, just to make sure. Nothing unusual happens.

Joy knocks on the door and asks if she can get in, says she's sorry about lecturing me. Um, I'm using the *thing*, I answer, and she says, Good for you, isn't it nice? and comes in to pee without wondering if I care. It is nice, I say, though the verbena foam is fading. A vinyl curtain between us, the soggy loofah rope around my wrist, I picture her bound up with her sister who lives in Montgomery, which produces some elongation. Terrified, I hold my breath until she exits, and force myself to recall a time before the desert. Joy remembers not to flush, which I love and appreciate.

Taped to the jar that held the ear was a weathered postcard of a black man, strung up above the manicured lawn of a historic southern courthouse. It was not our courthouse, but was quite similar, and the lawn featured a white marble statue of a soldier atop a tall pedestal, no doubt dedicated by the ladies of the town in the first decade of the twentieth century, just like ours was. In the picture, everyone seemed to be gathered around the marble soldier: the lynchee, men, women, and one little girl. The spectators were all white, though none of them looked rich. The hanging black body was beyond mutilated, and the face collapsed. People grinned from beneath. At these events it was not uncommon for men and their boys to penetrate the live body with corkscrews, extracting small tubes of flesh before the hanging. (They usually only cut the ears, nose, and penis off after death.) I hated it, just hated being so constantly at war: with a statue, a postcard, an ear. With love. Looking at Alex, I was devastated to think that by discussing the jar's significance I might infect him with my battle. Who was he to have to worry about the southern past? What else but sorrow would it bring him to question it?

On the one hand, statistically it just makes sense: since there seem to be fewer homosexuals than straight men, there would be fewer soldiers (hetero) distracted by sex, and thus fewer mistakes made on account of lust-based preoccupations. I mean, given the numbers, no women soldiers equals less lust, right? From the other side of the argument, I just can't fathom a bunch of fags wanting to rape their fellow Joes all over the desert. I stepped out of the shower and toweled off, then lifted the commode to stare at Joy's pee and tissue, and flushed. Alex asked if he should bring the ear to class to show what happened before civil rights. I said, No, and could tell that he was dejected. I felt bad and wanted so goddamn much to hold him. Instead, I told him that he should return the ear to the basement, and never speak of it again. Told him that, if possible, it was generally best to stick to the proven methods, advice which I believe we should all remember to remember, lest things begin to get away from us.

They

THEY SAID I had to do it. They drank Schaefer beers and ashed their Dorals on the apartment carpet. Cleared their throats and spat at the ceiling to make "stalactites" dangle. They were a few years older, more men than boys it seemed, and they told me there was no other choice but to take Lee outside and pound him. (He was in the bathroom down the hall when they decided this.) No other choice after what he'd done, they said. After all, that guy had been a guest in my mother's home, in *my* room.

In the dark of my room, his pallet on the floor beside my bed, Lee and I would whisper about everything, like brothers. He'd run away because of his father. Quit high school and hitchhiked all the way down from Chicago, and was terrified about things that happened to him en route. He confessed them to me one night, and I'd never imagined people doing such, and never again imagined men the same way. With every description his body had become more complicated. After that, looking at him was like looking at one of those old 3-D wiggle pictures, where two related hologram images appear from different angles. Clown with eyes open; clown with eyes closed. American flag flying; American flag with eagle. The boy whose body was consumed; the boy whose body was me.

Lee was sick about missing his sophomore year of high school. They said they'd get GEDs if they ever needed to, and then join the goddamned Army. The music in their apartment was always the same: screaming. They threw their empty beers at a tall, full trash can in the kitchen. Their living room was exactly like Mom's and my unit, only there was not a beige couch and small upright piano. There was instead a large Styrofoam cooler, several aluminum-frame outdoor chairs, and a wooden industrial cable spool used as coffee table. A Confederate battle flag tacked on one wall. The snot they spat at the ceiling desiccated into thin yellow strings that were as gnarled and brittle as worms on a sidewalk. The boom box on the floor had been taken as a payment. (They bought eight-balls of cocaine. They'd snort half, then stomp the other half full of baking soda, then stomp anyone who complained about being sold weak drugs. They'd ask me, Free cocaine, kid? and I'd say, No, thanks, and be nervous, and think about that nice cop who warned us about drugs in junior high.) They sported a gallery of tattoos, some incomplete. A forearm of half-inked panther; a flesh-colored Iron Cross amid a banner of crimson. They bragged about getting sex for blow from high school girls. They said I had to do it.

Mom had found Lee a couple of months before, in the laundry room on premise at our complex. He'd been sleeping in a hard plastic chair, his head down on folded arms across his bare thighs. His only pair of jeans in the dryer, the zipper scraping the drum. She woke Lee up to kick him out, saw that he was my age, and instead told him to get his gear together, to get on to our apartment for a bite and a bath. From there, a day turned into a week, and then he was just with us. Mom adopted Lee, sort of, because he was scrawny and put the plates away. Did chores while I was at school, and promised to re-enroll, ASAP, ma'am. He told her he wanted to go home but that his father, a senior chief petty officer, retired, would not condone him. Lee tried to dress tough, and would some-times borrow my boots. I once decided to walk in while he was taking a bath.

He went down the hall to take a piss. In his absence, they said he was a faggot, then called out, "Ohhh, Leeee-eee," in a sissyfied voice. When I didn't chorus in they said he was my girlfriend. I fumbled around for a way to deflect this, before blurting out, No way, y'all; that asshole made long-distance calls on our phone without permission; a whole bunch of them. (I was not angry about these calls, of course, nor was my mother.) Their response was that he was stealing from a single mom, and that I had better step up and be a man. They said I couldn't let people abuse me.

Lee came back from the bathroom and they laughed and said, What's up, faggot? and when his eyes dropped they said, Just kidding—lighten up, ha ha. He tried to hold a smirk. I was so nervous that my mouth got watery, like before vom-iting. He went to grab a Schaefer from the cooler and they said, Hey, give us some money for that, and Lee said, I don't have any money, and they said, Well, then you don't have any beer. They then looked straight at me and said, Want a beer, kid? and I said, Yes, and did not look at him. They winked and handed me one and they laughed and asked, How are we ever gonna drink all these fokkin' beers? Lee was bony, and I thought I could do it. They did not hurt inside. There's no way they hurt inside. They finally handed him a beer, then pulled it back when he went to take it, then gave it to him for real. Laughed when his fingers jittered with the pop-top, then looked at me and motioned that it was time.

My father's *parents* considered me a legitimate member of his family, though he had gone to astonishing lengths to avoid me. His lawyers had called me "one night and one bad judgment," arguing that his sole responsibility was to send my child support checks on time. Over summer break I would visit his parents, my grandparents, and stare at the photos of his other boy on their wall.

I thought of my father when I said, Hey, Lee, let's you and me go outside for a second. They snickered. He looked around the room, dropped his shoulders, and said, Okay.

I slid the patio glass door open and walked out into the overgrown lot behind the apartment complex. Lee plodded behind me, said he was going to go home on the Greyhound. Said he and his dad had talked on the phone a bunch, had talked of his joining the Navy after high school. I didn't respond, only kept walking through the tall spear grass, worried sick about how to throw a punch.

Lee said his dad was a hard-ass but all right, really. He then told me he wanted to go home.

My father's lawyers wore poplin suits. I wanted to try cocaine.

It was hot and dark out in the field, and the tall grass swished against our jeans as we walked. The framed yellow lights of the apartment fell away, and, convinced that the others could no longer see us, I stopped. Lee stared at me and started to mutter something pitiful, then trailed off. He cocked his head like a dog and turned up his palms.

I said, You stole from me, man, what the fuck? which didn't sound real.

He said, I'm, I'm sorry . . . I was calling my father, I've been trying so hard to—

I don't care, I said. My mother took you in and you *stole*. (I was still not angry, and wondered if anybody ever really was.)

Lee stepped towards me, arms out. Just let it go, he said. It's me, man. I'll pay you back for—

I said, Get off me, faggot, and shoved him, and this sounded more real, and he stared at me like I was a grotesque, a murder.

He said, You don't have to—, and I swung and hit his forehead.

Lee righted himself, repeated, You don't—

I stepped forward and hit him again. The blows were awkward, which made me try harder. Neck and head and cheek, again. Lee held up open hands. I demanded that he swing back.

He finally went down. I looked around, hesitated, then kicked him in the mouth. He curled up like a pill bug and screamed into his belly. I kicked him again, and again, until he finally shut up. I circled him. Spat.

As our panting subsided, he bolted up and ran off through the dark field. I crouched, and began to strike myself in the thighs and neck; I clamped my mouth shut with one hand and struck myself with the other, until I could no longer draw breath through my snotting-up nose. I took my shirt off and wiped my face, then slung it over my shoulder and walked back toward the light of the apartment.

Done? they asked when I came back inside.

Faggot spilled my beer, I answered. They howled in laughter and reached into the cooler and handed me another one. Feel good? they asked. I said, Sure, and slid my hands across my sweaty chest, as if I were sore or muscular. You know why he's not here, right? they asked, and I answered, What? because I didn't understand the question. You know why he's not standing right here with us? I tried to think of an answer but then just said, No. They snickered at this, said, He's not here because he's a bitch. A man would have taken his blows, walked back to the party, shaken your hand, and then got you the beer himself. Cunt, they said.

Bird (on Back)

AT DAYBREAK, A bird flew into our bedroom, smacked the wall mirror, and fell on Darla's back. She slept on. The meds really wipe her out.

Only minutes before this she was cheating on me, in my dreams. We'd moved back to the city, into a crummy third-floor rental. Darla was the only one of us who had a job (of course), so things were testy. And one night she went to a work party and never came home, and I sat on the apartment's worn linoleum for hours, frantic that she'd been killed, or run off the road by rapists, or everything else you can imagine that keeps you awake and a wreck in a dream. She came home the next morning, swearing she'd just been too drunk to drive.

We both knew she was lying. It was, after all, my mind. Yet the more I begged for reckoning, the more she clung to her story. "Take it. Leave it. Whatever," she said.

From the pain of this lazy lie I awoke, in our puny town, in the South. The room felt like a sweat lodge. The quilt was kicked to the foot of the bed, and the sheets beneath us were damp. I looked over at Darla, a vague ridge of shadows and dawn blush, and reached out to wake her for an argument.

The sound of the birds outside cut me off. A river, a symphony, I'd never heard anything like it in full daylight: layer upon layer of birdsong. Its construction made me think of my art, my process, and how I might capture this sound as diorama. For that matter, I wondered, what *is* diorama, when devoid of adequate light? When constructed primarily of sound? Can there even be an "-orama" without the seeing, the "di-"? Further, if my art can't be seen, then what control do I wield? Who *am* I?

I drowsed in ambitious creative thought . . . until something clanged from the other room. Bolting into the den, I found that Dim, the cat, had knocked out a window screen and fled. I figured that cat would be demolished in the street. I knew that Darla would blame me forever. I was the one who insisted the windows be left open, to save money on air-conditioning. I was the one who was unemployed—even in his dreams.

I was the one, always me.

I got back in bed and stared at the rose-lit ceiling. And THAT was when the bird flew through the open window, hit the mirror and fumbled onto Darla's lower back.

I was terrified that the bird's talons might break her skin, injecting some otherwise run-of-the-mill bacteria, and sending us straight to the emergency room, again. The bird, a big black one, stood up and stomped in place. Darla bore no thoughts of her sickness, or sepsis, or hospital; she didn't budge. If anything, she probably reckoned it was Dim skulking atop her like always, kneading invisible biscuits with its de-clawed paws.

Teeming with anxiety, I moved only my eyes. (Such self-control is difficult, you know, when a bird is pacing Darla's back.) It was a grackle, which I knew from many hours of looking at backyard birds while consulting the *Sibley Guide to Birds*, likewise scanning the book for birds I wished would visit Mississippi. It was missing one eye, and its feathers gave off a blue-purple hue in the sunrise.

Its dead socket stayed on me until I sighed, at which point the grackle whipped its head around, revealing a stark, corn-yellow eye. It cocked its head and blinked.

My God, I thought. What can I do?

I tumble around town a neglected dioramist. Though I constantly sketch, map, and *digest* every inch of our environment—town square to Yarn Barn to A.M.E. church, Civil War Memorial to Vanity Fair Outlet Mall—not one of the town's seven thousand residents has ever asked me, seriously, about my artwork. If the subject even comes up I am generally lumped in with the cousin who carves melon sculptures at the Dogwood Festival, or invited to some snoozy brownbag at the county library. I call my artist friends back in the city to complain, using an accent that Darla says is cheap and unfair and not even close. "'Varmints' abound in the South," I declare, describing hawklike mosquitoes and vole infestations. "Ever'body down here smiles while talkin' to you. But because they're smilin' they cain't be confrontational. No suh, you must avoid unpleasantness at all costs!"

My old friends laugh at me. They use their own shucks-y accents to describe southern stupidities that I've never witnessed, and I indulge this, and it's like I'm still with them, still a part of the scene.

In the city, Darla had been all mine (devotionally, not propertywise). She crunched budgets for young designers and had support groups to go to, and I had gallery representation, and site-specific commissions that would prop me up for months at a clip. Darla would surprise me with Zuni animal carvings bought from this Native American folk art boutique; I could easily find pancetta and cook us carbonara. In early spring, songbirds made nests in the tiny trees that grew in plots along the sidewalk. You would not believe how beautiful our life was, among the throng, insignificant. Strangers there didn't smile like maniacs, or stop you to remark on something pretty, or ask who "your people" were. They were simply mean or indifferent. Yes, the city drove Darla and me together, against the jerks.

I have found no job since my nasty split with the town's Oriental rug shop. A few weeks ago, I was passed over for a window dresser position at a women's boutique on the square. Though demoralized, I decided that the right opportunity would find me if I just held out, just held on. I shared this optimism with Darla when she got home from work. She tore her navy blazer off, said, "Gee, man, it must be tough having tons of time and no expectation. Thank god we can't have children." She then laughed at her own sorry situation, infertility being one perk of her illness.

Once a month we drive up to Memphis to pick up her regiment of pills, and to try and feel decent and anonymous for a few hours. There's a downtown garage called Parking Can Be Fun, and we park there, and it's not really fun, but just a normal city parking garage, bored attendants and tire squeals, the stairwells foul with piss. We park and pay and walk out into the bustle, and smell the dank Mississippi River, and maybe get overpriced Thai. It's lovely, this escape, façade, this dialogue with our first "term," which is what Darla calls our first four years together, in the city.

At the Walgreens here in town the pharmacists grin and say, Hey, y'all, and then whisper about us afterwards. On the town square or at Kroger's the residents smile as they sidestep us, pulling their kids in tight.

DARLA jostled, and the bird began pacing toward her head. It stared downward while doing so, like a philosopher. Helpless, I began to blame Dim.

We found that cat as kitten, in the city, beneath a '91 Toyota Celica in Chinatown. It was February, and an icy rain pocked the streetside mounds of snow. I had just stepped into a pothole of slush. My right foot was in shock, my Italian boots ruined. And Darla and I stood there, freezing, yelling at each other because she was immune to my complaints. In lieu of empathy, she mocked my fortitude and my manhood in her greedy slog for Peking duck; she screamed in that displaced southern drawl of hers until she was out of breath—at which point we heard this little *Graaaak* beneath the shred of sleet off of passing cars. *Graaaak*, we heard it again, and we figured it was a sickly bird, and we bent down and there was Dim, frail and drenched and hunched over her paws, the size of a bun under the rusty Celica.

For the record, I was the one who wriggled under the car.

(Also for the record, I wanted to name the cat '91 Toyota Celica.) Dim wants birds enough to bash out all of our window screens, but has no idea how to catch them. She springs when she should creep, yards away from anything. No doubt this is due to lack of kittenhood instruction or support—which I'm sure is also my fault.

THE grackle poked its beak into Darla's jumbled sleep hair. This was too much. I punched it in the face. It half cawed while slamming against the underwear drawer of our oak dresser, then fell to the floor. Darla shot up.

"What the? Honey, wha?" she asked, her fingers fanning her hair. "You okay?"

"There's a bird," I said, pumped.

"Where's Dim? Who bird?"

I pointed to the foot of the bed and we crept there. Peered over the footboard and saw it askew on the floor. Its good eye was half open.

"It targeted you," I said.

For a beat, Darla's face betrayed a soft look of fear. This was one of the looks I'd fallen in love with, six-ish years ago, when we were just friends of friends who'd never thought to fix us up. When Darla was provocative and brash, but still emotionally frail, her giddyup dynamism a smokescreen for the belief that nobody could fall in love with a terminal infection.

But I could, and I did. And seeing this look, this Early Darla worry, I couldn't help but clasp her wrist, smile, and nod to assure her. *I'm here*, I thought. *And I'm not going anywhere.*

"What have you done?" she asked, pulling free.

"Done, nothing. There was an eyeless bird on your back."

"Bull-shit, man," she said, naked except for striped panties. "I see its eye right here."

"Yes, but . . . but what would you want me to do, Dar?"

"Well, for one don't murder anything!"

"It pecked your head! It was awful, like those beast-walking birds on Animal Planet. On the . . . *veldt*!"

She reached into her mussed hair, confused, perhaps relieved—until the bird blinked.

"For heaven's sake," she said. "It's a bird."

"Grackle."

"Whatever. Where's the cat?" She got out of bed. Those striped panties of hers had a cute little sag in the bottom.

"Dim must be out," I said. "To let this happen to you."

"Out? Jesus, man, I'll find the stupid cat." She marched toward the den. "You take care of that bird."

I shut my eyes and sought power, then reached to stroke the bird's mangled wing.

"Please," I whispered. Its beak parted when I touched it. I blew on it and it blinked. "Please die, bird. Die before Darla gets back."

BEFORE all of everything there was Darla and her Greek Revival mansion. She's a Mississippi native, which is why she took up the offer from her folks to move us back down here after the city got too exhausting. When the energy it took to navigate choked the energy it provided, and, according to her homeopathic hippie nurse, kept Darla's viral load jacked up. Yes, we moved to this self-styled arts town, which we'd seen showcased in the city paper's Sunday magazine, written up as "quaint" and "affordable," and which had made her homesick. She promised the place would be to my surprise, that I'd have space and time and money to make my art. That it was warm, and that the people were extremely friendly.

And it is and they are—always.

Though I've yet to visit her parents' home outside Jackson, Darla once told me (over much wine) that her mother, called Miss Sally, keeps a room full of dead babies. That Miss Sally's got somebody inside the women's clinic, the last one open in Mississippi, and that every time a woman aborts, this spy-nurse gives her an eight-by-ten of the pre-procedure ultrasound. Darla said every inch of wall and counter and end table space in their upstairs study is covered with X-ray babies; she said it's Zygote City, that the images are in silver frames her mom snaps up from Stein Mart and Marshalls.

Miss Sally had each frame professionally engraved, until it got crazy expensive. Now she goes to PetSmart and has the instant engraving machine print the date of procedure, the names she gives the babies, and a fit-able version of the God talking to Jeremiah quote—*I knew U B4 I knew U*—etched onto twilight-blue dog tags that can be super-glued onto the frames.

When Darla was growing up, her mother made her tour the shrine every Sunday after church. Miss Sally had her read the names and dates aloud, then explain to all why the world had treated them so poorly, and how things had gotten so bad.

Her father, Walker J., would insist that he be allowed to memorialize the aborted in his own way, dear, and then light out to ride the back nine at the C.C. of Jackson. Douse himself with Dewar's and spend the night on his leather-and-tack office sofa.

Whatever. Darla still got a convertible BMW for her sixteenth birthday.

She met the soldier who would infect her over spring break, sophomore year. Throughout our relationship I've seen him in every uniformed guy. In every war movie, every tribute, every stupid soldier commercial. Woe, the battle-bruised warrior. The remorseful kid-killer. The one-night-stand hero whose viral dick still dictates our life.

We could have broken his hold early on. All we had to do was lose the condom: In the city, in Darla's huge clawfoot tub. In the exposed brick bathroom that was roughly the size of my bedroom, its fifteen-foot ceilings and frosted-glass daylight. The tub where she told me the story of that soldier, the twenty-something Army man with the overburdened heart. The one who Darla had wanted to heal, as she'd been taught was a thing to do, as generations of her family's women had done for their defeated southern men.

Yeah, we were in that clawfoot, lounging across from each other, our arms on the tub lip and knees cocked up, she making sure not to spike herself with the spout, and . . . and the wakes of rippled bathwater, the drips off of our elbows as we reached for our beers . . . the spatter on concrete floor and wet rings from the icy bottles . . . when I realized that we only had to fuck, unprotected. I told her this, and told her, truthfully, that I'd never adored anyone before, and that I was desperate to join her body forever, to charge the field of her mortality and wrest back control. For both of us.

Her refusal to let me is like a snapshot I can't stop staring at. I still can't believe she chose that soldier over me.

DARLA stomped back in the bedroom and started throwing on clothes. "What are you doing to help?" she barked. The broken bird remained in a heap on the floor.

"Baby, please don't be so mad," I said. "I was only looking out for you. I mean, have you thought about histoplasmosis? That's the condition Bob Dylan had in the sac around his heart. It's no picnic of a disease, and folks say it comes from *birds*. Birds that . . ."

As I detailed the havoc of histoplasmosis on her shitty immune system, Darla nudged me aside, mumbled, "I am so, *so* sorry, bird," then picked it up, sighed, closed her eyes, and snapped its neck.

I gasped.

She stared at me, eyes welling. "Oh, come on. Didn't anybody ever take you hunting as a kid? You never winged a bird? Had to take responsibility?"

I shook my head no, horrified.

"Course they didn't. Why would anyone teach anyone to be merciful?" She held the flimsy bird up, and started to sob. "You think that was easy?"

She walked off and tossed the bird into the master bath trash can, grousing through her tears about life lessons and urban wimps. She then brought the can in and put it on the floor beside me, before going to scrub her hands. (The Waterless Pumice Hand Sanitizer is bolted to the bathroom wall because Dillon Chemical won't make anything smaller than a gallon dispenser. The sound of her smacking the plastic nipple on the bottom gets me so flustered. She refuses to consider using any other scent besides Dillon's Bayberry Breeze, even though she knows I can't stand the smell of it, likewise that there are a bevy of pseudomonacidal, salmonellacidal, fungicidal, and virucidal cleansing scents to choose from. I constantly clean up her vomit, from bedside floor to underside of toilet rim, rarely giving back so much as a stutter because I adore her, and because vomit has no place in love. Still, nothing but Bayberry, Jesus Christ.) She threw her hand towel at me as she marched out of our bedroom. Seconds later, I heard the back door slam.

I stared down at the bird, in state, in its final nest of old floss and tissue. I supposed that given all the violence, Darla had in fact brought it mercy. Deliverance. I had no idea what to do with it—bury it? chuck it?—so I just put the garbage can on top of the oak dresser and looked elsewhere, again.

To be fair, the thing about the birds in the city trees is that there isn't much protection from the elements. Unlike the lush growth here, those trees are more like sticks with veils of sprig, so spring winds knock the nests to hell. In April, the urban sidewalks are littered with fallen hatchlings, their chicken skin and bulbous purple eyes. The buried trash of an entire cosmopolitan area emerges with the thaw, and next thing you know, there they are.

Darla was back within two minutes, scratches on her face and Dim in her arms. She looked at me, sitting on the bed, and then saw the can on the dresser. She flung the cat onto the floor, where it writhed in the ghosted bird's scent.

"Follow me," she said.

"I'm paralyzed. But you should clean those scratches up, quick," I said.

"Come on, now."

"You'd better—"

"Now!"

So I got up and followed her, through the living room and kitchen and den, and back to my art studio (the garage). She banged the fluorescent lights on, and shook her head at the burgeoning diorama.

"Darla," I said. "You can see the progress I've been—"

"Tell them," she instructed, pointing at my village, the landscape of which took up most of the room.

"Tell them what?"

"You know what," she said.

"How is it that you're the one from the South, but I'm the one that understands these folks?" I asked. "You can't just *tell*. Nobody *tells* down here. They just smile and pretend like everything's perfect and gay."

"Tell them what went wrong with us!" she screamed. "Explain how things got so bad!"

"Well, um," I said to the unfinished chaotica of small-town façade, to power tool, paint and plywood scrap. I cleared my throat for *they*: the miniature postal clerks and student-baristi, the genteel abortion doctors and half-painted pastors and proud teenage miscegenators and roadside retriever mixes. "Ahem," I said, to not one goddamned soldier. "We moved down to Mississippi for the air and the restfulness. Darla has autoimmune issues. Surely you've heard of rales or rhonchi? She should really not have a cat. She was stupid as hell when she was younger, but is smarter by sexual default now.

And me? I'm a heel who doesn't understand, who apparently doesn't have to do anything, ever, and who is therefore the sole drag on her life. The heel outsider with normal blood counts who won't take any stupid job, and who never meets anybody or contributes to any stupid anything. Who is frozen by the past. Where she loved *him* more than me."

I turned to her, "That good, babe?"

"Always has to be about you," she said, and walked out. "Always, always," she repeated down the hall.

I stood there, furious and guilty and sweaty, which oddly enough struck within me the desire to complete the pivotal scene from my current project, working title *Township*, which I hope will reflect a sort of postmodern dialogue with—or as response to?—the world's largest diorama, the Cyclorama, in Atlanta. Based upon my final day clerking at the Oriental rug shop, and contrary to the Cyclorama's depiction of the entire Battle of Atlanta during the Civil War, to the *entire Battle of the South*, really, the focal point of *Township* is an Ordinary Guy who stands up to Power. It takes place in the rug shop, and can be pictured thusly:

An upscale southern woman is patting her bald, tiny-headed baby, which hangs in a decorative sling over her shoulder. My boss, Mr. Dempster, a wad born of plantocratic stock, is explaining to the lady that an antique Heriz rug is in fact a treasure, despite the toughness of the wool and relative lack of dense Knots Per Square Inch (kpsi). I stand next to a stack of rugs, idle and silent, prepared to showcase another nine-by-twelve as cued by Dempster's nod. The diorama woman swats and seems to be saying, *Well, the rug is lovely Mister Dempster, but all said and done I'm concerned about the central medallion.*

The piece has to . . . She sways, sashays almost as she talks and swats, which is why the dioramic baby is vomiting/has vomited on the parquet floor. Accordingly, this is why the onus came upon me, as clerk, to wipe the milky vomit up.

When complete, my defiant pose will indicate that I've said: *I'll get you some paper towels.* Mr. Dempster's counter-pose will indicate that he has corrected me: *No. You'll GET some paper towels.*

The problem, in terms of portraying the resulting tension to Darla, to the world, is how to edit-in all this action, which continues/continued as: *Oh,* the woman replied, aghast at the thought of wiping the vomit up herself; the baby's bitsy head jostled, at the time driving me to conclude that if I were ever to sculpt a baby with a head so minuscule, it would be—and thus is now—deemed a disproportionate flaw (unlike portraying vomit, which may be imprecise); I walked to the back of the store and unraveled many paper towels from the spool, something I'd long gotten used to when cleaning Darla's vomit at home; old popcorn was on the break table in a red plastic basket lifted from Chicken City; a stare-down ensued upon my return: the woman at Dempster, he at me; I stared at the baby and the vomit, and held the towels out for whomever would take them; nobody took them; the baby slung about, looking elsewhere; we were all at a crossroads, and my chest grew heavy as I again thought of Darla.

In the Alley That Runs Behind My Rotted Clapboard Apartment House There Are Sick Cats

IN THE ALLEY that runs behind my rotted clapboard apartment house there are sick cats, everywhere.

No. That's drama. Mostly, they're healthy. A clowder of lithe kittens not yet smashed by the low-riding thugs, or mauled by neighborhood dogs, dogs that crap by my back door.

But there is this one old queen. Her fur is the color of the street-plowed snow. Gunky ruts streak from her eyes, and the end of her tail is hairless, like a rat's. She's the only mature cat I've seen around here. Is Chicago's queen regnant of Hermosa and Humboldt Parks.

I looked for her the other day, after Spec's makeshift IED blew house paint and hot sauce over the driver's side of a parked BMW. Within thirty seconds of the blast, half the neighborhood leaned out of their open windows. Aroused by confusion, their breath tufted in the winter air. It took three minutes for City of Chicago's first responders to arrive, though a full two hours before the bomb squad had cordoned off the street. (This neighborhood is far more Hermosa than Humboldt, so the saving arrives in degrees.) In the interlude, many of us went outside to gawk, the young snapping selfies while wrapped in dramatic parkas, the old clobbering the cops with accusations of neglect. Having recognized the construction of the IED itself, I just looked for the old cat. As the pinky mix bled into the cavity of shattered side windows, I wondered if she was ready for what's coming.

Fourteen degrees, late November, I find her tugging turkey bones from a fallen trash can. The foil that wraps the carcass scrapes the alley ice. In the four years since my out-processing from Bragg, having abandoned a return to Tennessee for the unknown of Chicago, I've never gotten near her. The cat pivots in precise opposition to my approach, her eyes fixed on me, her tugs convulsive. This is straight-up terminal endurance. It reminds me of an anti-world: urban ops, Baquba. Where high-rises meet skin- and scab-colored streets, and scars of charred sand and metal, and bricks like hailstones and sinews of rebar from pulverized terraces, and black spray-paint warnings on bullet-pocked walls. The plotted oases of palm trees and rushes amid the browns and blacks and bloated.

The fact is, that cat should die. I know this now. God knows it. You look into her eyes and realize that even *she* knows.

Enough spirituality. Woe-ish anthropomorphism. In the alley behind me, kids chuck bricks through the back windshields of parked cars. Did it again the other day, just below my kitchen window. Afterwards, I ate a ham sandwich and watched some hipster white girl cry into her phone while pacing the rear of her Subaru. From the rooftop of his catty-corner brownstone, Spec filmed her with a handheld, his face shrouded in black balaclava. At some point he noticed me in my window, lowered his camera and stared. I offered a slight wave, then held my right hand to my heart, Islam-style. He considered this, the snow dusting his black mask, then turned and disappeared.

Through the alleyside chain link, the kids poke sticks at old dogs, stabbing them in the gums when they bark. I yell at them to stop and they call me faggot and *maricón*, *puta* and bitch. It doesn't bother me. The faggot stuff. The dog stuff does. I watch them hurl empty bottles against eroding brick walls, and sidestep the security cameras of the rehab-condos that flower around us. They dump over trash cans and wait for the race-modified Japanese cars to blaze through the alley. They taunt each other and yell like kids are supposed to, and dare each other to break windshields, and burn dope and get worried about kid stuff and Chicago public school, and walk and brag about their older brothers' beat-mean dogs. Presa Canarios. American Pits.

We are under invasion. The horde of others buy and rehab the clapboard houses and small brick buildings, the refuse dragged through the alley in dump trucks, a hemorrhage of exhaust. In the early evenings, after work, these others cruise our neighborhood, gathering intel; they scout and evaluate and buy and sell the structures—the kids' families still inside. Sometimes they skip the rehab altogether and just raze. Hired guns block off parts of the sidewalk with yellow tape, and then pickax the Slavic inscriptions off of the worn stone archways. Mercenary pickers strip the copper wire and piping, careful to crimp the gas lines, to always crimp the lines.

Or not. Mostly, these invaders merely patrol in pairs, in German SUVs, talking to each other but doing nothing immediate. They scout for the big red *X* that the city of Chicago bolts onto dilapidated buildings—indicating that public resources, e.g., fire trucks, should not waste their time.

(Third strategy: The invaders scout, buy, evict . . . and then just sit on the empty houses. The kids and families are thereby redeployed: two blocks south, six blocks west. The windows and nooks and alleyside crannies of the empty homes are boarded over; the buildings sit in waiting for the black and Puerto Rican and Polish holdouts to turn over the rest of the grid.)

Sometimes, men and boys hire on to help destroy their own spaces. This, too, I saw in Baquba.

The pickers must crimp the gas lines so the buildings don't explode. So the gas pockets don't mark time for a spark.

In my tiny kitchen, on the bistro table beneath the window, is the application. It sits there, day after day. My VA home loan can or will buy a fixer-upper. I can or will play a part in an undeniable future. I can buy this place, or the one next door, and rent to artists or grad students or . . . anyone who will wear this neighborhood like a medal, like a badge that indicates their life at the edge. This was the same dynamic in Nashville before the war. Hell, I think it was the same thing in Iraq.

SPEC is twenty-two or twenty-three, Latino, still at the point where he dons his dress greens for church and on Veterans Day. His Specialist 4 rank insignia and campaign medals are

Brasso'ed and perfect. At least, I *think* this kid is Spec. He doesn't go by that nickname, anyway, certainly not to me. On warm summer Sundays, he'll loiter on the porch with his parents. The old folks on adjacent patios or porches call hello to him in Spanish; the drive-by crews nod out of respect. If and when I have tried to engage, hurling a question or comment from my stoop to theirs, Spec falls silent, or just walks inside. His mom will jump in to rescue the awkwardness, her accent and Spanglish a bridge of neighborly communion.

Sitting at my window, I like to spy on him through my old combat optic. Tickle him with crosshairs as he engages the empty houses, setting up his snares and traps. Other times I sit on my front stoop and just watch him tend his stupid dog. Dare him to confront me.

Spec can't let go of war. What's worse, he remains idealistic. Instead of contemplating his own VA loan, trying to buy in or buy up, he risks all by planting snares inside any building with a lockbox. Coyote spring traps are set to snap metatarsal through Italian leather loafer. In the gutted brownstone hulls he mounts plastic buckets full of shit and orange soda above cocked doorways. He tags the building exteriors with hobo code, lest the kids or locals fall victim to his devices. A rectangle with a dot in the center, or a symbol that looks like a *T* tipped on its side. I can't translate the signs but I know what they mean.

I also know what comes next: the Surge. Spec knows this, too, that law enforcement will soon mobilize against him. Yet he still posts raw phone video of a Hakkotsu shock grenade explosion from down the street. (He introduces the online segment on a makeshift set—his bedroom?—while clad in a Bulls' ball cap, shades, and black bandanna. On the wall behind him is a modified City of Chicago flag, in which the flag's three central stars have been replaced by dollar signs. Spec issues conditions to the authorities, the banks, and the gentrifying rich, then calls out neighbors who stride the fence.) He rigged the Hakkotsu inside an empty Big Gulp cup. Detonated it just as a female realtor unlocked a gut rehab for a young Indian couple. The latter sprinted off. The former squatted to the sidewalk in a piss-wet skirt, her fingers toggling her ears to clear the ring.

THE dark grooves beneath the old cat's eyes are pure sick. Distemper rivulets, blood and influenza. I wish she would die. In the alley, when the kids walk their Pits and Presas, and that one fat Rottweiler, she flees. Pulls her nicked ears back and hauls ass, like a refugee, or jihadi. She looks proud, somehow, sometimes. The young cats invariably end up crushed and ice-matted, their blood-rimmed nostrils and gaping mouths.

Outside my hazy kitchen window, rising from the horizon of flat rooftops are a pair of antiquated, rust-iron cupolas. Remnants of a neighborhood not under siege, they're the only structures I've learned to appreciate here. In the afternoon sunlight, they remind me of Rome.

EARLY in my time here, one evening at sunset, I heard a car pull into the alley below my window. It stopped and idled brusquely, as if it had a hole in the exhaust. A few seconds later came the report of five or six low-caliber gunshots. Tiny pops, cutting the atmosphere. This sounded like cheap fire-works, or like those plastic mini-champagne bottle streamers so rampant in everyone's Chinatown. I ran to the window to assess, my father's old M1911 pistol in hand.

Christ, Tennessee, I thought. You do NOT engage com-bat outside of an official combat zone.

The car gunned it back to its own eroding neighborhood. This was no militia. It was just a rival gang. Cats and kids scattered.

I can never relate the fury: torn awake at 3:21 a.m. by the back-and-forth of a rapid-fire, low-caliber semi, and the slow cannon blasts of a large-bore revolver. Exactly as the con-tinuity of the firefight drove me to the floor, consumed by memory, the gunfire ceased. Things fell into pitch, homelike silence—until this rock-star-confident male bellowed, "*I hit you yet, nigga?*"

THE kids will kill the old cat if they can. I just want to cure her. Replace her. In Baquba and Taji, they were everywhere: legions of runny-eyed runts, available to absorb rage. Yet nobody messed with them. Rather, they just lived, and bred, and mewed, and no local kid or old man yanked them up by their tails. Booted them to feel in control. Amid the palm rows and beige buildings, the onslaught and block-to-block, it was as if those cats were neutrals. Better than neutrals, though, because all sides sort of revered them. Tacitly. Tiger-striped kitties pouncing as if on cutesy YouTube—against a backdrop of torched cars and rubbled mud-brick. The fetid stink of the Diyala and orange groves and burnt plastic, people.

YOU don't need much money to see Rome. You only need take advantage of your earned combat benefit. If things get too intense at home, you claim space-available on a DoD flight to Baltimore, then on to Aviano, and Rome. You stay in this Philippino-owned rooming house, surprisingly close to Piazza Cavour. Share a *residenza* with strangers and cook for yourselves. You don't have to go on tours or buy expensive clothes. Just saunter around, lost in the antiquity, amid the sun-soaked spectrum of pastel-colored walls and lame political graffiti, plant-lined terraces and umbrella pines. Hike up one of the hills and sit through dusk. Buy food for the cats from a cart at the Forum.

MY mortgage broker called last week. It is time to pull the trigger, or reassess; by spring, this block will outprice me. I listened, and listened again, my eyes fixed on the neighborhood of questions that populate the VA app.

Late that night I put on my black fatigues, then snuck into Spec's target homes and removed all of his devices. I left the snares and spring traps in a box on his doorstep. I trust he will realize this more as tribute than threat.

LATE spring through early fall, when you come home at the right time, at the first cast of sunset, you see it. Generations gather around the stoops and doorways, and laugh and yell and wave. The old ones tell embarrassing stories about the young while sweeping smooth their Astroturf patios. The young ones take turns practicing rhymes, cheering or jeering each other's performance. Spec looks on, smiling. When I was very young I lived in a small decent house in Nashville proper, in a would-be historic district hemmed in by squalid urban housing, and I was afraid to go outside, and was told not to do so when alone, and inside that house I one day saw an old video for a Rolling Stones song, "Waiting on a Friend," and Mick and Keith and a couple of Jamaican guys gathered on the steps in front of a gritty metropolitan graystone, and all kinds of people walked by, and Sonny Rollins played saxophone on the soundtrack while they hung out. This street reminds me of that, only that is a joke. This is a double-parked Ford Explorer with a Puerto Rican flag hung from the rearview mirror by golden tassel, and with lowered windows from which erupt a sonic mash of hip-hop and Latino rhythm that wiggles the hips of young and old and me. It is the sigh and squeal of air brakes on the bus at the corner. It is a squirrel standing upright beneath one of the city-planted trees, her teats bursting with milk; it is the fair-haired Polish barber-woman who shuffles by after work every evening, rolling her eyes at the dark-skinned newcomers (who have been here for at least a generation). The smell of the take-home pierogis she clutches, the punk lottery tickets at everybody's feet. The cautious, peering eyes of an orange kitten beneath a parked car, and the crepuscular sunset, purple, pink and navy, drenching a ceiling of clouds like quilt batting, my god.

□   □   □

I can never relate the brutality: 4:17 a.m., awakened by the Ophelian babble of a young white woman. I lay in bed, staring at my ceiling as her whispers rose into garbled questions, then rose into sobs—and, finally, into mindless, screaming pleas: *"Help me, please. Somebody. Help Me, Please. Somebody. HELP ME! PLEASE! SOMEBODY!"*

Alongside anguish, the woman's cries also conveyed a plain-as-you-please disbelief that absolutely nobody cared. Cares.

As she stumbled beneath my alleyside window I ran into the bathroom. I tried to vomit, but couldn't. I couldn't call the cops either.

SPEC has this German shepherd with smashed hips. You can tell the dog's injury is a couple of years old by the way it hops. By the way its pale tongue hangs, and its eyes hit the ground. Spec has to yank the dog outside by this harnesslike device made of old belts and duct tape. He cinches it around the animal's neck and chest—taking the weight off the back legs— then lifts it up by the duct-tape handle and lugs it down the front steps of his building.

Dog looks like a piece-of-shit suitcase. Placed in the strip of sidewalk snow, it ambles sideways, as if drunk. Spec stands beside it and smokes while the shepherd coils around, then quakes as it defecates. He looks away from the dog, and to the industrial FOR SALE sign, red letters on white, newly bolted into the side of his house, a rental.

I'd be embarrassed if it was my dog. Spec doesn't acknowledge the disfigurement. He just flicks down his smoke when the animal finishes, yanks up the silver-tape harness, and lugs the shepherd back up the front steps. Goddamn dog. I bet it used to be the most gloriously mean motherfucker in the alley.

LAST night, drunk, coming home from the VFW on South Wallace, I emerged from the train to a neighborhood on lockdown. Nobody walked, loitered, cruised; there was nothing but the sound of the train gears squeaking away, then the flitter of tumbling trash. I shuffled past shuttered liquor store and Title Loan, Carnicería and Orthodox Church. Stapled to power poles were new Health Department signs in Spanish with a picture of a target over a cartoon rat's head: *Ratón*. I cut into the alleyway, leaned into the razor wind, and marked progress by yellow streetlight spheres. I imagined an insurgent rupturing my capillaries, his fists bashing the blood vessels of my sclera. I knew that I was being watched, yet there were no beautiful neighborhood kids to save me, to serve as witness. No romantic cat analogy. No war narrative to claim.

No. That's drama. There was and is exactly one war narrative: Benefits, rightly mine. Health. Retirement. Education. Home ownership. Cheap meals at Applebee's on Veterans Day. Ten percent discount at Lowe's.

The rest of it? The cause? The memory and terror? Sanctimony. Total bullshit.

I clapped my gloved hands and laughed at myself, my boots crunching bottle shards as I walked towards my dog-shit-littered alley door.

Stepping through a cone of security light, I heard a series of metal clinks from the adjacent darkness. I darted into shadow and crouched against a wall, grasping for a rifle I haven't carried in years. I keened to the source, a black void of open crawl space, a haven of cats and gas lines.

"Spec?" I whispered. "Specialist?"

Nothing.

"It doesn't have to go down this way," I stated. "I mean, think about it. There are guerrilla garden plots to plant. Or we rehab the neighborhood rec center. Or . . . or hell, man, let's occupy a red *X* house. I mean, just take it over. We'll occupy, then gut and rehab, and then give it away to an evicted family. Teach the kids how to do the same, then unleash them on the neighborhood. We can fight, Spec. Can retake the land. And your house, even. We can buy your house proper and establish a base of . . ."

From the crawl space came the waft of rotten eggs, of the mercaptan fused to natural gas. "Specialist? The opening of gas lines is not an acceptable tactic. In fact, this is selfish, a shortsighted campaign. And you know what? I get it. I do. I know what it means to stand next to death. I crave how it feels to be made alive by violence. But it won't work like that anymore. Not here, anyway. I promise you, man. The law won't turn their backs on this. It'll take about a day to figure out someone blew this building up, and another to figure out it was you. And then?"

Still, nothing.

"Spec?" I called out. "Let me in. Please."

I waited for a few seconds, then turned and marched home. On my doorframe was a newly scrawled hobo symbol. A diamond shape with a line pointing up from the top corner:

A diamond on a noose? A diamond with a fuse? Whatever it meant, there was no mistaking the threat.

"Roger that!" I shouted, then spat into the blackness. I went inside, sat at my lighted table, in my lighted kitchen window, and filled out that VA loan app.

THIS morning I woke to a rhythmic clash of metal on metal. It sounded like a chain gang, or the grinding track gears on an APC. I got up, put coffee on the burner, looked out the small window, to my Hermosa and Humbolt Parks version of Rome. Two brown men in layers of plaid flannel shirts were tearing down the first of the ancient cupolas. Blue-sky-blue surrounded them. The process of destroying both domes took about an hour.

I dread the idea of walking up on the old cat's carcass. Best-case scenario, one day, one week, I'll realize she's gone. This will be enough.

Colleen

LAND

COLLEEN LAY AWAKE the nights, staring at the popcorn-textured ceiling. Her bedroom window was propped open by a box fan, its draft blowing out against the thick Mississippi air. She smoked in slow, labored sighs, a glass ashtray on her tummy as she sprawled on her old twin bed. Now twenty-two, she'd gone from high school straight to Basic Training and AIT, then on to deployment, before circling right back to that rural, postwar starter home, and to her childhood bedroom, a chorus of graduation tassel and sapphire-paneled basketball trophy, her parents biting back the demand that she smoke outside.

She'd get her own place soon. A job and whatever. Sometime.

She could picture the desert, barren and pocked by missile char. Fighter jets rented the vast gray horizon, cracking the sound barrier, shredding the calls to prayer. She had watched them deliver payload on the beige city in the distance, a city almost shorelike against a gulf of sand, and with minarets capped in turquoise. From her platoon's staging area she saw the explosions, and the tufted clouds that rose silently afterward. At distance, it took several seconds before the concussions of the blasts had arrived to buckle her knees; the space between visual and physical was like being stuck in a riptide, a schism of cause and effect. Colleen could not get over this dead interval. She was terrified of it, but more than anything wanted to find it again. To somehow crawl inside.

The beige city in the distance. The goat herd that wandered onto the edge of the formation. Their bellies distended, their hip bones propping hide. Gray and black goats with stringy beards. Their shepherd, a lanky teenage boy in a beige caftan, wielded a dry reed. His face was smooth and feminine. One troop had laughed about the goats acting like stray dogs, trotting in a pack, starving, their dusted tongues bobbing from the sides of their mouths. Their shrill bleats and neck bells. Starving and trotting toward the soldiers.

Colleen and the platoon had loitered in the sand, having exited the vehicles despite orders to stay put, to remain on the outskirts and wait. They were heavy with equipment, tactical armor to tempered steel plate; their sweat was quickly shed to the oven-dry air. The guys pissed at the back bumper, and cut up, and listened for the order to engage the city. Now and again they'd seen the small, muted blooms of smoke rise from a frag grenade or IED.

They had spot-welded scrap metal to the floorboard of the Hummers. They had not live-fired their A4s. They were staged at distance from the action, on the periphery, waiting. And the goats had charged at them for food. And *pop-op-op*, brass casings hit the sand. They dropped half of the herd within seconds, and then Colleen and Van Dorn and the rest of the squad had held the shepherd kid back at gunpoint, his face a squall of *Why?*

This was early in the tour. They still held indoctrinations of faith, honor, manhood, love, remorse, reunion, memorial. Yet after the episode, the simple killing of goats, Colleen had sensed something sensational about herself, about all of them: They were free. Of obligation, code, or history.

Of land. Day upon day, staring into the void of sand, surrounded by it, coated in it, the talc-like granules circulating in her lungs, deposited, expelled, she was divorced from her lifelong relationship to land: how it had defined her, and her parents, and even how earth itself had been defined by others before she was even born. How the passing down or manipulation of soil determined both who you were and what you weren't.

Yet looking across the desert, ridiculous in its capacity, all direction marred by only what was temporary, truck to tent to trailerlike CHU barracks, to the drift, even, of landmass, the dissolution of history by wind, Colleen understood that for the first time she was rendered landless—but with total authority. There was nothing to accumulate, to pay down, to pass on. No demarcation, save sand and rock and horizon, and the ability to navigate it at will.

The void was lawless, and gorgeous with opportunity. They were able in theory and by firepower to traverse the space as deemed fit.

It was strange to her that the majority of her unit still stoked the narratives that they felt relied upon them: the things they owned or could potentially own; the foods they had always eaten, or the women and kids who depended on them. The talk was not of transcendence, but of combat pay and mortgages and church; of the predetermined highways that would guide their new, postwar pickups. They yammered about GI Bills and VA loans, and the fixed-rate rewards of making it home in one piece.

Again, this was early on. By the end of the tour most of them didn't care if they ever redeployed.

One morning, a few months into that first tour, Colleen had requisitioned a Deuce-and-a-Half truck, then veered off of the asphalt two-lane and into the gut of the desert, alone, carving the sand, fishtailing wildly. She looped the vehicle a time or two, marking great quarter-mile circles, and then cut deeper into the expanse, weaving in snakelike curls. Her vision and hands forged new pathways with the wheel; her tires left ruts where none had rutted. She ran out of gas in the middle of everything, and then watched the sand-drift devour her tracks. She was scared. Thrilled. She wriggled out of her clunky, ill-fitting body armor, and she squatted and pissed in the sand. Laughed so hard that she teetered onto her backside—and then laughed even louder, and applauded for nobody.

The roads, she thought now, as she stared at that popcorn ceiling. "The land," she whispered as she looked to her pink bedroom walls.

She got out of bed, and tiptoed across the room. Chewed on her thumbnail and looked out the window, to the moonlit pines that walled the edge of the property. In memory, she again heard the bleating of the goats, the hobbles, the *pop-*

op-op. She remembered the balance of the herd trotting over their dead.

They had given the kid a wad of USD for the damage, joked, "Get along, now, little haji." When he had continued to protest they waved him back with rifle barrels. Corporal Van Dorn then razor-wired a nanny to the hood of the Humvee.

Picturing Van Dorn made her eyes well. Colleen shuddered, and wiped her palms against her cheeks, and then rocked on her heels to try and strangle his memory—though she knew this would never, ever happen. She smoked another cigarette, and stared at the lighter. She flicked it and flicked it, then hurled it across the room.

CRIED, BEAT EACH OTHER

SHE had come home on a chartered United 777, landing at Fort Bragg after a stopover in Ireland, a layover at an airport terminal full of whiskey kiosks, and with windows that showcased a green landscape shined by rain. It was the loveliest place she'd ever seen—a judgment aided by the daze of jet lag, and the lens of the Occidental: lipstick, skirts, 3-D movie ads. Colleen, swollen with optimism, swore she would return to Ireland one day . . . if she could remember the name of the town.

Stepping onto the tarmac back at Bragg, she felt nothing, save annoyed. Everyone else's lovers and wives kept bumping into her. They carried handhelds and placards, and children who wagged tiny American flags. They knocked her about, not even an "Excuse me," as she cut across the steaming black asphalt, looking for recognition.

Her mother stood in back of the melee, in Dress Barn denim, crying. Colleen walked up and accepted a too-long hug, and was told that her daddy wasn't there because of work, because the fields back home were snowing in cotton.

"Of course," Colleen said. She wondered, though, if maybe her mother, Janette, hadn't encouraged this arrangement. Or, conversely, if her father hadn't tempered his own desire, in order to let the two vets share their moment.

Janette hugged her several more times, and then returned to the crusty, base-side motel when Colleen's unit was beckoned to their barracks. She told Colleen that she was going to stay for however long it took to finish things up. That they would drive back to Mississippi together. Janette then insisted that Colleen name the food she had missed the most, and Colleen couldn't really think of anything, because missing food was a frivolity that had vanished months before, when the actual missing of anything could no longer be satisfied by shit concept or dream. When pushed, Colleen threw out that the catfish plate from Cracker Barrel would be awesome, thanks, and Janette said she'd bring one back ASAP.

The subsequent communion, a to-go catfish dinner on a weather-beaten picnic bench, soggy batter and Sysco-esque bins of tartar sauce, was meant to bridge a lifelong rift. The squeak of plastic fork on Styrofoam, the straw-suck of sweet tea and the sticky glaze on fried apples brought the brokering of her mother's own National Guard deployment, Operation Desert Storm, 1991.

"You know, Mama, you never talked about your mobilization," Colleen said.

Janette glanced up and smirked, then stabbed at her fried okra. "Well. You were a toddler when I was called up. Too young to understand what—"

"I could feel it, though. After you came home. Always."

"That's dramatic," Janette said, rolling her eyes. "Hell, Colleen, my greatest regret is that I joined the Guard even though I was plannin' for a family. That I spent a year of my life gone. I cried every single day over there, then smothered you with hugs when I got back."

Colleen said nothing.

"What?" Janette asked.

"Only two times I remember you even talkin' 'bout the war, Mama. One was the screaming match you and Daddy had after you refused to attend church in uniform for Veterans Day. Two, when you gave me your campaign service medal after we lost at regionals, seventh grade."

"You were so good at basketball. Why didn't you pick it back up in high school?"

"You said I was your hero," Colleen continued. "And Mama, you pinning that medal on my chest was awesome. But, like, that was it. That was *all*."

"Well. Just try and—"

"I still feel shut out by the silence. The specter. The feeling that Daddy and me was holding you back. Were keeping you held—"

"Hey!" Janette barked. She stared at Colleen, then reached over and patted her hand. "There was just *nothin'* I could have told you about war. Nothin' I could say. You know that now, right?"

Colleen stared at her lap.

"Wadn't about you, babe," Janette said, then opened the Styrofoam boat that housed their dessert. "You know that now."

They moved on to commentary about double-fudge cake.

Two days later, Colleen told Janette to go on home, that out-processing was going to be another week of standing in line, of hearing tests and head evals, of forms and forma- tions and who knows what else. Her mother assured her that it was no problem to wait, and asked Colleen if she wanted to talk.

"Naw. I'm good," Colleen said. "Promise."

They left it at that. Janette hit the road.

That night, Colleen and her squad went to the base PX, and bought handles of whiskey and tequila. Within an hour the guys were pissing on the hedges outside the white clap- board barracks, and, jokingly, on each other. Two guys from the motor pool beat each other to pieces, then got up and hugged, and cried, and pushed their foreheads together, blood smearing, then clacked their bottles and swapped I-love- you's, and everyone else called them dick-lickers. Colleen and her cohort had laughed at this spectacle, because they needed to laugh, and more so to hug and kiss, and even more so to demolish each other, to make sure the hugging and kissing didn't spread.

The lot of them then decided to go into town and lay waste some whores.

The club in Fayetteville had been loud, smoky, name-less. Beneath the drench of knockoff perfume was an air of mop water and puke. Uniformed were everywhere: drunk, loud, immortal. They were immune, still, to the bill cycles and family reunions, parent-teacher meetings, gas prices and cuckoldry that would quickly re-latch and debilitate.

Colleen sat at a small lacquered table while her squad members embarked with various shades and shapes of women, in and out of tiny, makeshift rooms partitioned by floor-to-ceiling curtains. They'd laughed at her as they left her alone; "So sue me," they'd say, and then ask her to wish them luck. She did. The whores periodically came around to Colleen, and asked her to buy them a round. She did. The women hung around long enough to brag about their ability to make anyone happy—wink, wink—and Colleen grinned and was flushed, and looked to the table but said nothing. The women moved on. She sat alone and stared around the room, and drank. And drank.

At some point a couple of way-gone roughnecks, Airborne, arm in arm and staggering toward the door, stopped at her table. They stared down at her, their heads keeled to the side like confused dogs. Seconds later they burst into laughter, one falling to his knees in hysterics while the other giggled through an apology. "Really. We're sooo glad you're here," he said. "Like . . . hoo-ah, sister!"

Colleen betrayed no expression. The roughnecks laughed harder at this, their rage and amusement so clear on their skin, their combat so real through their diaphanous skin. They laughed at her until a grizzled first sergeant came out of nowhere and shoved them out the door—deaf to Colleen's protests that they be left the fuck alone; she didn't need any son of a bitch looking after her.

During the brigade's final day of out-processing, she informed her CO that she would no longer drill when they got back to Mississippi. She told him to transfer her, no questions, to Inactive Ready Reserve (IRR), whereby she was no longer responsible for any Army anything, save waiting on word of her honorable discharge and VA benefits. He agreed to this. The CO had heard rumor of what happened between Colleen and Van Dorn back in theater. He'd heard enough to know that things would be simpler without her.

She signed a handful of forms and the war was done. She got on the bus back to Pitchlynn, Mississippi.

AT NIGHT

SOME months after redeployment, Colleen was in a dark room traced by the odor of sweat and cologne, and maybe semen. She and the boy kissed a little and then she broke off laughing. The red glow of alarm clock digits spread across the white dorm refrigerator, which she opened in order to take another beer. The boy leaned in and bit her neck as she gulped. His hands then slid over her, grappling her breasts, and she wobbled over and rested against what she guessed was a large padded recliner. A La-Z-Boy like her father's, situated across from a television, as was his. The beer can on her lips, the boy's lips on her neck, she stared at the slip of white hallway light at the bottom of the door, and she thought about her CHU trailer at forward ops, about the hairline fissure

of light that had poured over the tall concrete barriers outside, and into a crack between the corrugated metal wall and
corrugated housing of the air-conditioning. She remembered
being lodged in that trailer, hour after hour, ordered to wait,
to stand down, practicing Arabic commands while aiming
her M16A4 into the mirror—*La! Ogif, shithead!*—listening to
small-arms fire and to the men mobilizing outside, packed in
too tight to pace, too tight to scream, the fracture of light was
salvation, a way out.

The boy turned her and walked her backwards, until her
calves hit the edge of the bed. "Hold up, grunt," she said,
teetering. She drained the beer and dropped the can on the
linoleum. She giggled, then pulled him onto the mattress.
His breath was a fashioning of alcohol and smoke and fading spearmint gum, and his fingers fumbled to unfasten her
bra. She guessed he wasn't more than three years younger,
probably less than two. Yet he moved with the inept, throaty
greed of a fifteen-year-old. Colleen refused to let this bother
her, mostly, and finally reached back and popped the bra
clasp for him. He said nasty things and she ignored him,
wanting only another beer. His t-shirt came over his head,
and then hers the same. He clenched her dog tags for a second, without recognition. She stared at that strip of white
hallway light and tried to remember how she'd picked him
up. She marked the smell of unwashed sheets; the feel of a
handed-down comforter sent from home. He moved on top
of her, nearly muzzling her with his mouth, his hips and
penis grinding into her. She reciprocated to a point, the
puddle growing inside, aching, her body soon wetting his
fingers.

▫ ▫ ▫

SHE'D spent that morning at the Veterans Administration Outpatient Clinic, Pitchlynn, Mississippi. It was her first time visiting the converted Motel 6, and she had since determined it her last.

Under the clinic's gum-colored portico, two passenger vans had idled, waiting to shuttle the fucked-ups to the big VA hospital in Memphis. The van's civilian drivers had cut their conversation in order to ogle Colleen's approach. Her eyes hit her feet as she stepped past them and through the sliding doors.

Coughs, wheezes, wheelchairs on commercial carpet. Beyond the reception desk, middle-aged and old men loitered in clumps, reeking of body musk and tobacco. Synthetic-blend jeans and nylon jackets, insignia on black baseball caps, had memorialized their service.

An hour later she'd been lying to—no, *corroborating with*— the VA claims investigator—who grilled her for one, tiny complication of her tour. Physical or mental trauma. Anything they could claim.

"Surely there's *somethin'* you can hang your hat on," he'd prodded, his wiry steel hair and pilled black turtleneck. "Some kinda pain worth anything?" His paneled office wall featured a poster of a Stryker vehicle. A plastic ficus tree was wedged in one corner, its leaves muted by dust.

(A Stryker, Colleen remembered. Bodies on bench seats, crammed and jostling, the wheels crunching landscape, the lull of engine strain and the rhythmic clash of gears. Your helmet clacks the armored panels behind you. Clacks the helmets of the troops sitting on either side. Heavy with web gear, mask, Kevlar, weapon; the air-conditioning always out, the cooling vests not worth shit, you can't believe the constriction, the hour after hour in 125 degrees. In 130, 150, gulping water, so much water; everyone but you can piss without removing body armor. Banging along, pressed against each other, their cock tips dropped into empty Gatorade bottles, sweating, unable to do anything but listen to the chatter of the driver and the M2 operator, trying to dodge the cube of sun blaze from the open hatches above. Sweat and gears, and the trembling need to piss, the consideration of pissing in your BDU pants, terrorized by shame but having to piss so bad you buckle in contraction, so bad you can feel the first blossom of tract infection, and you pray for the strength just to wet yourself. All of this alongside the constant, practical concern about what faceless object will kill you. Not if, not when, but what.)

"Think, girl," the man had ordered. "Let's get paid."

"I," she had whispered.

He cocked an eyebrow.

"The, um. Warts?"

"Gotta speak up."

"Plantar warts?" she'd asked. "My feet are still screwed up from them boots."

"Warts!" The investigator laughed into his lap. "We can work with this. Now, if we was talkin' Vietnam, hell, it'd just be part of the deal. But today?" His pen slashed at the appropriate form. "Warts it is."

She had come to the VA seeking counseling. Someone to

talk to. Someone who could explain and then exorcise her compulsion to hurt, to trash herself, to do whatever she could to get back to the elating brink of trauma; to random, visceral, adrenalized trauma.

But you couldn't just walk into the walk-in clinic. You had to go through the process like everyone else: intake paperwork, biomed overview, financial evaluation, wait; benefits categorization, primary physician assignment, claims screening, wait. Instead of seeing a shrink, or even a nurse prac scripting SSRIs, Colleen wasted half the day being humiliated for her postwar weakness . . . then shamed into filing for a payout over warts.

Leaving the claims investigator's office, she'd been dispatched to give blood and urine, meeting the requisite demand of a physical before her claim could be filed with the federal government, perhaps as an action *against* the federal government, in part because the Feds gave out unnecessary handouts. This was Mississippi, of course.

Meanwhile: wait.

The men who sat around her in the VA clinic lobby were black and white, using canes or in wheelchairs, their pajama pants legs tied in a knot. Elderly wives in cheap wigs sat beside them. The Weather Channel beamed from a wall-mounted television.

They stared at her. She sat in a row-bound chair, adjusting her legs, her ass and her everything, until the clerk finally called her number. He gave her a plastic cup, and pointed to the unisex restrooms. She went inside, noting the chrome handrails by the toilet, her nose sorting the communal bodily smells. Read the posted instructions on how to give a sample: Wash Hands Thoroughly Before Touching Penis. Pull Back Foreskin If Applicable. Urinate for 3–4 Seconds Into Toilet. Do Not Touch Penis to Interior of Container. Fill Container Between ¼ and ½ Full of Urine for Doctor.

She pissed on her fingers and knew she'd contaminated things. Wiped herself off and tugged her panties up, and then stared into the mirror until the urge to cry had passed. She returned to the clerk, placing the sealed urine cup on a Tupperware cake tray at the edge of his desk. He ordered her to wait, said they'd call her in an hour or so for the blood draw.

"No worries," Colleen responded, and marched out the sliding doors. She drove to the string of cheap bars near the campus.

CAST in the seam of hallway light beneath the dorm door, she flipped herself from under the boy. They peeled their clothes off, and she mounted his thin frame. She positioned his erection behind her; he struggled to place it inside.

"No," she ordered.

"Condom?" he asked.

"Christ, no."

She moved her pelvis in a slow, circular rhythm, her hands palming his hairless and slightly muscled chest. She pegged him a high school sideliner, only recently divorced from dreams of further athletic pursuit. He groaned and again tried to penetrate. "No," she repeated, moving atop him, circular and fluid. She reached between her legs for a few seconds, then used her self-slicked hand to cradle him outside of her body; she rocked up and down, his penis gliding between her buttocks and wetted palm. Slipping against each other, he so desperate to enter, she so intent on rupturing this need, so insistent on receiving the pleasure, the puddle, as generated by only exterior heat. His cock lodged tight between her hand and buttocks, Colleen bucked back slightly so that her vagina remoistened him, her hand stroking him as she rode up and down. Her climax began in waves that radiated outward, downward, inward as she grasped him, the tide of elation moving her to spasm; her pelvis backing into him, her gasps her kneaded breasts her hand sliding faster, up and down and up and . . . The tickling warmth on her back as the boy came in an apex of deprivation.

He gulped like a child. She shushed him and gripped his involuntary pulses.

Buried in the darkness was the sound of a tiny gear. Colleen knew exactly what it was. Because every troop seemed to have taken the same shots: Vehicle, sand, mortar fire; helicopter, sunset, the Coke logo in Arabic. Interiors of CHU barracks, blast scenes, bloated dead goats and hajis . . . as frequently cut by the automatic shutter closure of a dead lithium battery. The tiny rev of a camera gear. Click.

(She had no idea that war and campus were conjoined by a love of slut-shaming.)

She got one good punch in before he covered his face, and another few about his neck before he threw her to the floor. She was silent as she got up, focused on finding the device in the pitch-dark. She kicked open the small refrigerator, using the light to check the closet. He called her a white-trash bitch, and considered forcing her into the hallway, where she'd be poised for ridicule by the brothers. His eye closing from the punch, he instead covered himself with the comforter.

She found the camera hidden in bunched clothes atop a hamper. She threw it against the wall, splintering the darkness with the scatter of plastic shrapnel. He cursed again as she grabbed her clothes and stormed out. She ducked into the men's hallway bathroom, dressing inside a filthy stall—her bra and panties and one sock absent—then marched back into the hallway, toward the exit. When the boy's face peered out from behind the metal door she kicked it into him, and he howled in pain. She flew down a flight of stairs and through a large front room, a space defined by worn leather couches, by crest-like insignia and Greek letters on the wall. On a large flat-screen television, *SportsCenter* chattered away for no one. She marched out of the house, between the white columns and onto the front walkway. She did not know the campus, and was unsure of how far it was back to the bar, and her car. She had not remembered to grab the memory card. She marched past the genteel university buildings, wondering how many more nights out she could take. Headlights passed over her, those of SUVs mostly, stuffed with drunken, privileged kids, kids that were her age give or take, a few of them teasing her clumsy stride. Her footfalls were hobbled by plantar warts. Her shirt clung to her back.

VFW

COLLEEN pulled into the oyster-shell parking lot of the VFW, then killed the engine. Buried by moonless night, she sat and listened to the snap of the flags in the hot breeze, American, POW, state flag with stars and bars, and to the clank of the metal fastener and guide rope against the aluminum pole. She lit a Misty.

The building looked more like a machine shop than a clubhouse: blue corrugated exterior and white metal door. A quartet of pickup trucks dotted the lot, and a trace of country music seeped from inside the canteen. She had passed the hall all her life and never paid it any mind. But she couldn't do another night at an in-town bar, in Pitchlynn or even Oxford or Tupelo. Another morning coughing up phlegm, reeking of stranger.

She wore her desert boots and a denim miniskirt. She paused as she reached the building, took a deep breath and pulled the door open. Stepped into the tight room of damp, orangey light. The walls were adorned by dime-store trinkets and bumper stickers, guide-on pennants and cardboard crosses of Malta. Walking toward the bar, she watched herself in the large mirror on the wall behind it. She saw a handful of good ole boys with beat faces, whose VFW caps lay flat on the bar by their drinks. There were black plastic ashtrays and a small television in the corner. Fox News, muted. A thick drift of smoke.

They stared and waited for her to ask for directions, or maybe to ask for her boyfriend. One of the men, Vietnam-era, bit the side of his lips. The bartender, tall and gray-bearded (also Vietnam, or maybe Desert Storm), nodded at her. The few elderly men, Vietnams, maybe even a Korea, looked to the television, or into their drinks.

"Help you, ma'am?" the bartended asked.

"Wouldn't mind a drink."

"Uh-huh," he said. He looked to his colleagues, as if wanting someone else to reply. "Um, darlin', I don't mean to be unkind. But you know we's a private club, right?"

"Yeah," she said. "I know."

"Well."

"Well?" she asked.

"Guess you're a vet?"

She nodded.

He lit a cigarette. "We appreciate that. And we glad to have ye. But the thing is, you have to join up. Not just qualify, see?"

"Didn't know that part," Colleen said. She nodded, and started to turn back to the door.

"Hell, Edwin," one of the men said. "Give her a goddamn drink. She's earned it."

The bartender pinched at his ear. "Sure. Yeah. But after tonight, you'll have to apply, okay? Ain't some social club. You'll, uh, have to apply."

She pulled a stool from the bar, ordered a Jack on ice. The room was mostly quiet. One of the men looked at her. "Desert?"

"Yup."

The men talked of the coming harvest, of Southeastern Conference football. They smoked religiously, the exhalation clouding a string of red Christmas lights that ran along the bar shelves. Colleen ordered another drink, then another. She chimed in on their conversations of farm equipment, and cursed harder and with more flourish than their wives or mothers or daughters. With whiskey-watered eyes and rounded consonants, they found that the binding link between all was the stinging legacy of plantar warts—a recognition that had them all guffawing. Someone suggested Colleen might like to apply to found a Ladies' Auxiliary. She figured that she was qualified to join any VFW post—Ladies' Auxiliary or not—and considered stating this. But she also gauged intent, and let it slide, Thank you, and then ordered a round for the house. The men raised their glasses.

Beyond the drift of the recorded pedal steel rose the sound of car wheels skidding outside, and the thump of bass from a loud stereo.

"Aw, hell," the bartender said. "Here comes our newbie." The men snickered. The Maybe Korea paid his tab, noting that he was gonna get out before it got too wild. His body just couldn't take it no more.

"Y'all still got all that crazy in you," he said to Colleen. "Still don't know how to be home."

She smiled and shrugged her shoulders.

Corporal Van Dorn walked into the bar, desert boots on the floor, a boisterous How-dee! to all in attendance. She turned to face him and he froze for a second, before breaking into grin.

"No way," he said. "Thirty-fuckin'-eight? Whatchoo doin' here, girlfriend?"

Colleen turned back to the mirror. Van Dorn walked over, sat at the opposite end of the bar, slapping one of the men on the back. "What damned cat dragged ole Three-Eight into this joint?" he asked. "She's a sight for soreness!"

"She ain't no thirty-eight years old," the bartender

responded, handing Van Dorn a Bud Light. "Looks about twenty to me. I mean twenty-one!"

"Naw." Van Dorn snickered. "It's a joke we have. Right, Three-Eight?"

"Sure," Colleen said.

"Thirty-eight is the MOS job number for Civil Affairs," Van Dorn explained. "Desk jockeys. Now, y'all geezers don't recall that because you never had to consider chicks. Army puts most of the girls in Three-Eight to keep 'em safe and shit."

"So you's Civil Affairs?" one of the men asked her.

"No."

"Just a joke." Van Dorn snickered. "Right, Three-Eight?"

Colleen turned up her drink, and nodded for another. She lit a cigarette, the flame of the lighter quivering. A couple of the men asked Van Dorn how he was, and he held court as he blustered and bragged. They tolerated this, because story-telling—his or anyone's—cued up the opportunity to indulge their own tales, to again revisit their trauma.

So the men did just that, they ran a story cycle, memory to memory, barstool to barstool, and on down to Colleen.

Van Dorn snatched the silence from her. "I tell you one thing y'all ain't never seen, and that's a woman in full web and chem gear, middle of a combat zone, tryin' to cop a squat!" he bellowed, and some of the others chuckled in response. "Hey, Three-Eight? You remember th—"

"You so interested in stories, why don't you go on ahead and tell 'em?" Colleen asked.

"How's that, girl?"

"Go on, hero," she said. "Tell 'em about us. 'Bout you and me, and what we done."

"Huh-oh!" One of the old vets snickered. They turned to Van Dorn, eyebrows cocked in wait for steamy detail.

"Hell, Three-Eight," Van Dorn said. "Nothin' to tell."

Colleen sucked her cigarette, and watched the ash flare in the mirror. She slid one hand to her lap. She could picture the cubes of sunlight through the small APC inlets. Could almost feel the weight of his torso, heavy, his body pinning her against the vehicle's padded bench seat, his hands cuffing her wrists.

"Come on, stud, tell it!" she barked.

"Whoa, girl," the bartender said. "I think maybe it's time we—"

"I said there ain't nothin' to tell, Three-Eight," Van Dorn fired back. "Nothing in the world I can tell these men about war that they ain't already lived. I mean, look around you."

The bartender continued, "I think our new friend has had a bit too—"

"Who do you think these men are?" Van Dorn asked. "What don't you think they know? Hell. You think they don't know killing? They know killing. You think they don't know heartbreak? Terror? Torture? What on earth am I gonna tell *them*?"

Her eyes watered, so she stabbed her fingernails into her palm.

"Shit," Van Dorn continued. "You know what, though? I guess I could tell 'em what it is to have to stare at a blood spot on the ass of your fellow troop 'cause she's up and run out of

Tampax. Remember that, Three-Eight? Huh? Guess I could talk about having to stare at stupid brown roots growing out of dye-blond hair. About having to negotiate combat while flanked by someone verifiably weaker than you."

"Anything else?" she asked.

"Woman with hairy legs? They prolly don't know about that. That the kind of thing you want me to talk about?"

After it had happened, she'd been unable to confide in anyone. She had walked around camp bowlegged for days, wearing no undergarments. When she could no longer stand the pain of mobility, Colleen had claimed flu to get off of rotation, then stayed on her cot for most of a week. She did not eat much, and she was silent, and she swabbed herself with aloe vera sunburn gel.

Staring at Van Dorn, she still couldn't understand why.

"Was I the first?" she asked. "Or did you burn other girls?"

He looked at her as if she were crazy. "Like I said, girl. Nothin' there."

The men jostled around on their stools. One motioned for another drink.

Colleen lifted her glass. "Okay, I'll get you started. So we're in the Stryker vehicle, just you and me. And I don't know about you, Van Dorn, but the fact that you were supposed to, well, *babysit* me 'cause I wasn't supposed to engage in combat was a bummer. Pissed me off, bad. Still does."

"True, that," Van Dorn said. "I was—"

"Shhh. Hold on, I'm settin' the scene here!" Colleen waved him down, and a couple of the men chuckled. "It was kind of a blur, all so fast. 'Cause I tell you what, Van Dorn, when you pounce, you're quick, man."

He sipped his beer.

"Oh, and y'all, that vehicle *stank*." Colleen looked at Van Dorn. "You smell sour, dude. And your chin? I can still feel your stubble scraping my neck—ugh. And, let's see . . . Oh. The screams. My screams in that goddamned Stryker were intense, right? Couldn't even hear the firefight. Couldn't hear nothin' but me screaming. Hell, *I* even wanted me to shut up!"

The bartender cleared his throat to try and break the story up.

"And my god, your erection!" Colleen said. "Now, there's a short story these men haven't heard. Your erection, still in your pants, pokin' all up against me while you pinned me down. I mean, one minute you're one of us; the next, your little pecker is jabbin' all over me!" Colleen forced a laugh. "You wanna take it from here?"

Van Dorn stared at her.

Colleen rolled her eyes. "Okay, be a chickenshit." She continued, as if setting up a joke. "So, boys, he's pinning me down, right? He smells like a sow and his boner's poking all over creation. And somehow, despite everything I'm still, like, *Okay, here it comes. We all know what's up. This troop is gonna do his biz. Gonna rip my pants off, and then his down, and then he'll spit on his fingers and la dee dah, whatever, right?* I'm thinkin', like, *Let's get it over with, Stinky.*"

"Sorry, gal," the bartender said. "This isn't the type of—"

"But this crazy mother didn't even unbuckle his pants! Shit, y'all, he just shoved his hands down my panties and, no kidding, um . . ." She blinked back tears for a second, then caught herself. "I mean, I thought an IED blast had seared us from beneath the vehicle! It burned somethin' awful down there! I flopped like a fish on a bank. Flailed so hard I threw him off of me. And guess what?"

Nobody answered.

"This perv had a Zippo lighter in his hand. You believe that?"

Nothing.

Colleen snickered, sniffled. "Yeah. Like, he didn't even wanna *rape* me. He just wanted me on fire."

(Afterwards, she'd pushed her BDU pants down to her knees, and peeled off the rayon panties that had melted to her pubic hair. When she wailed like an animal, Van Dorn screamed for her to shut up, saying, "Jesus, I's just fuckin' around." The air in the vehicle was clotted with the smell of singed hair and flesh.

Colleen had lain on her back, on the bench seat, rocking, bawling. She'd been confused when Van Dorn gently handed her a bottle of water, then stared as she doused the blisters. "Just fuckin' around," he'd repeated. Gripping the corrugated black plastic of his rifle barrel, he began to bang the butt of the weapon against the Stryker's metal floor, ordering: "You"—*bang*—"calm"—*bang*—"the"—*bang*—"hell"—*bang*—"down"—*bang*. "Now!" In the silence that followed, he smoothed her hair with his fingers, muttered, "I barely even flicked.")

Through the bar's smoke and neon, Colleen stared at him. She wished to god she'd had the old Browning .22 her father taught her to shoot with. She'd inhale, hold her breath, line up, squeeze. Squeeze, squeeze, squeeze. Center mass, as the Army commanded. She figured Van Dorn might even laugh when he saw the .22. Might hold up a hand and charge her, convinced of his ability to absorb the rounds in his palm. All the better, she thought. All the better he forget the kinship between her Browning's 5.6mm bullet and the 5.56mm round of the carbines slung in theater. Forget that the U.S. military chose the minuscule 5.56 round for a reason; forget that instead of a fist-sized cavity left by an AK-47, that counter to any Cold War profundity, the sole intention of the 5.56mm round is to ricochet: off the bones, sinews, spine. Forget that you can in fact shoot a man in the legs, or the ulna, and the round may well bounce all the way into the abdomen, shredding muscle and artery. She'd give it all to him, center mass just as trained, secure in the pinball-like reflection of the bullets inside his rib cage.

"That about right?" she asked him. "Anything I forgot?"

Van Dorn looked to the mirror behind the bar. The men turned their eyes from his reflection.

"What I thought," Colleen said. "Anyhow. I'll just let you get back to tellin' these boys what a badass you are."

She fumbled in her skirt pocket for her keys and some money.

"Hey?" the bartender asked, startling her. "You good?"

"Well," she said, pausing to consider. "I'm better."

He nodded. "I hope so."

She threw a $20 on the bar and walked to the door.

"Come see me," the bartender called out. "If you need to talk or somethin'."

Within a minute Colleen was stomping the gas pedal, kicking up a hail of oyster shells as she peeled onto the county road. She was drunk, and the car drifted across the yellow centerline now and then. No matter; she was heading deep into the countryside, nowhere near anything, let alone a cop. The clean night air pushed like a river against the mildewed odor of the Cavalier. The tires squealed as she took a curve, and her headlights flashed over vast fields of row crops, cotton and soybean and corn, and the endless steel trusses of center-pivot irrigation arms. She was not Civil Affairs. It didn't matter what her job was, anyway. She held an intimate knowledge of every weapon at the company's disposal. She could break down and clean and refit and reassemble any standard-issue rifle—SDM, A4, M16/AR-15, M203—any of it, faster than anyone in the battalion. M60 and .50-cal. "What the?" She pounded the wheel as the tears came, then gunned the accelerator, the car lilting as she hit the dips in the road.

Her life was pinned between Highways 7 and 15. It always had been; whether as a child riding to town with her father, or on the middle school bus, or while tooling around with handsy high school boys. Her homeland had been carved up before Colleen was even born. Driveway to asphalt, highway to interstate then back again, she ran on a track forged by someone else, by men; a map, a guidance system, a grid, thrusting her from point to point, repeat, repeat, the cycle punctured only by trauma.

She whipped the Cavalier off the road at full throttle, thrusting into farmland, nearly rolling the vehicle. The tires threw gravel, then dirt, and then the windshield was gummed with plant life. Young corn stalks lashed the window frames, their row spacing a drumroll, their shorn silks and tassels, confetti. She then steered the vehicle into wide arcs and curls, exactly as she had in the desert.

As the car shaved the crops, its engine near redline, Colleen knew that nobody had ever forged that particular pathway, in that particular way. She laughed at the landlessness of it all, at her authority in motion, and then yelled out in glory with the choir of snapped stalks . . . until the Chevy smacked dead into the irrigation tower and her face cracked the steering wheel.

Blood streaked her chin as she processed the pain. She listened for fighter jets, or the bleating of goats, her muscles locked in anticipation of a blast concussion.

When nothing came to engage, Colleen let go of her fear. She lay her head on the wheel as her body went slack. Her consciousness drained out to the wobble of gooseneck pipe that spanned the quarter-mile sprinkler truss.

She wasn't dead. She was twenty-two years old, and very much alive.

11/19/98

This unusual episode is one of the series' best ever, with the non-stop comedy roller-coaster suddenly throwing a brilliant surprise ending at you.

—"THE ONE WITH ALL THE THANKSGIVINGS," from *Friends Like Us: The Unofficial Guide to* Friends

ANOTHER GLASS OF Beaujolais Nouveau. Every year, Shea tells me how special it is. Every year, it tastes terrible. Finally, this time, this year, at the Whole Foods I asked her to buy a new California wine instead. Called simply "Nouveau," it was positioned right next to our horrible stuff. I mean, great marketing. It was from Sonoma too, I think, which would've been pretty good. (After all, Williams-Sonoma is pretty good, right?) The debut Nouveau also had an artistic and flashy wine label, just like the French stuff. Beyond even Beaujolais, the fake wine came with Christmas-ornament grapes in bronze patina, noosed around the bottleneck, for free.

Shea didn't go for it. She said that some traditions are just that—traditions.

Anyhow, it's Tuesday. It's Wednesday. It's Thursday. Must-

See teevee. *Friends* and co. at six o'clock, six-thirty *Seinfeld* noosed around its neck. I'll get another glass of this crummy wine. "Shea? You want anything?" "No, thanks, hon. Six minutes!" God bless her, lounging on the weathered brown Italian leather of the retro Cotswold sofa. The ruby Pakistani rug at her feet—what's that rug pattern called again?—by way of Nieman's. Resto Hardware oak coffee table, matching end table, bronze patina lamp and knickknack closing in. The laughable Burberry pajamas by seven p.m. The skin-tag polyps in her armpit. Another glass of wine.

Here's the kitchen, here's the wine, *Access Hollywood*. I need some wine. Kitchen. Should have gone with the Viking stove, for resale. Or at least the FiveStar. The rust-colored, Italian-style, Mexican-made-tile so slick under sock feet. Countertops wiped to a gleam. The cobalt-blue triple-Moen-sink; the green digital numbers of the stainless microwave. Travertine abounding, and Sub-Zero fridge, stocked. Museum of Fine Arts *The Impressionists* magnet smack-dabbing photo of Shea and me from the newspaper's About Town section. I bought the Jenn-Air stove but was wrong to do so, despite what I argued to Shea and later had to admit, no problem. The Jenn-Air was $2,701, cheaper than Viking—ridiculous. Now I notice that 2-7-0-1 comes up all the time, just to mess with me. Like, there were zero commercials shown on 1/27. No kidding. Instead, at every break the network ran news clips of the President saying, "I did not have sexual relations . . ." So depressing. And of course 12/07 is the "Day That Will Live in Infamy," year after year. Point being, the Jenn-Air does not have (a) the resale value, nor (b) the conversation value of the Viking. Or even the FiveStar, for that matter. And since we're not going to cook anyway, well, what the fuck? We need all the resale and conversation value we can get. Yes, I'll be the first to admit it. My mistake. I hope we've moved on.

"Honey?" she calls. "It's about to start"—12/71 being her birth month/year.

"Okay, coming." I am hungry, am I? We've been watching for years and years and years and . . . since right after college. This and *Seinfeld* and *Frasier* and, well, things have gotten interesting. *Seinfeld* and *Frasier* are the new *Cheers* and *M*A*S*H*, rerun- and real-episode-wise. Five-thirty *Seinfeld*, six o'clock *Friends*, six-thirty *Seinfeld*, nine-thirty *Seinfeld*, ten o'clock *Friends*. Seven o'clock new *Friends* and *Frasier* on Thursday. Shea and I joke that if you flip the remote exactly right, you never have to hear a single syllable of Peter Jennings or Dan Rather, or anyone else depressing. The other evening, around five-thirty, she said, "I'll trade Chandler Bing for Vernon Jordan any day." I said, "Ditto me for Joey Trib instead of Linda Tripp!" Do they still show *Cheers* and *M*A*S*H*? No? Maybe, yeah, sometimes, where?

"Honey?" I call to her. "I've got one."

"Uh-uh, here we go. Better be good." A few times a week, Shea and I do this thing where we'll claim exterior-only parts of each other that we love.

"It is," I yell back. "Oh, hey—can you hear me? Hold on a minute."

I think I should piss. Moen faucet in bathroom, icy granite, extra-deep basin. Silent-flush, cavernous bowl. For a while, the whole Phoebe-gets-pregnant story line on *Friends* was hard for us, but the show is just too funny to stay down about. We try to do the thing where Shea pulls her knees up to her chest after I come. We'll see. I despise the doctors, the specialists. Mostly, we never know whether to be excited or depressed when Shea doesn't get her period. I can't even ask her anymore. Textile-linens from Monte-somewhere in Italy, via Neiman's, which are supposed to be "exquisite," but really don't sop up all that much. Bed, bath and shower curtain. (Still not sure if a downstairs shower is good resale or not.) The preview of today's *Friends* Thanksgiving special says they'll all remember their Worst Thanksgivings Ever—which I guarantee you will come up for a laugh around the table next week, at Thanksgiving. Aveda Energizing Body Cleanser and Aveda soaps promise "the art and science of pure flower and plant essences." What the hell? Woman stuff, I suppose. Shea raves about this crap. I got a pimple after using it. Hadn't had a pimple in years.

I call to her, "Okay, ready?"

"Ready as I'll ever be," she says with a laugh.

"The backs of your front teeth," I announce.

"Really?" she asks.

"Yeah, really. I mean, unless it doesn't count. Does it count? Wait, you don't have to tell me. But I think it should. And you know what?"

"What?" she asks, smiling as I walk in, zipping up.

"Even if it doesn't count I love them, okay?"

"No. I think it counts," she says. "When my mouth is open."

Today's episode airs on 11/19, a sibling of 11/91, which was when I came home from combat deployment. I was 19. Shea was there, waiting. I'd sent her weepy letters. She'd watched CNN. And of course there's 9/11, the date G. H. W. Bush formally laid out his plans for war. (Ugh, I'll never forget it, 9/11/90, because as soon as he gave the speech I got this sinking feeling. I just *knew* our unit would be mobilized—which sure enough it was, in mid-November, 11/90—heck, maybe even 11/19/90. I'll have to look. That would be too weird.) Next week, Thanksgiving is on November 26—1-1-2-6—the exact last four digits of my Social Security number. They won't show a new *Friends* episode, which is totally depressing.

Bokhara. That's the rug pattern. It's Pakistani, and mostly red but with small golden octagons in two rows, lengthwise. Real soft. The wool has great lanolin content. The guy at Nieman's told us the octagonal shapes were supposed to represent elephant footprints. Crazy.

It was difficult at first to try and deal with the Must See evolution: Where was regular *Seinfeld*? Where was Thursday night? (And where did *Cheers* go, anyway?) When they first started messing with the whole lineup, specifically when *Seinfeld* bailed on us, it felt like things might fall apart. No kidding. I mean, what happened?

Miraculously, we've only become thicker. Richer. This is partly due to the fact that *Frasier* is now on Tuesdays, in *Seinfeld*'s old spot. Also, Shea and I are trying to put our faith in *Jessie*—the new show between *Friends* and *Frasier*—because of its decent premise and time slot. *Will & Grace* is . . . well, *was* an odd one to get used to. We weren't sure if we'd be into faggot comedy. In fact, we were pretty sure we wouldn't be. (Plus, this whole Shepard-boy-Wyoming-thing with the barbed-wire fence is a super-downer.) But they're hilarious! That one little queer guy is just so queer that there really isn't anything to worry about. It's not like he's trying to sneak up behind you, you know? Plus that other guy isn't so gay all the time. And, as Shea points out, Grace is hot.

What's next? We are hungry. Are we? Wolfgang Puck's frozen pizza, four cheeses? Lean Cuisine? Amy's vegetarian burritos? Uncle Ben's bowls? "Honey," Shea calls. "Can you bring me the throw when you come in?"

"The what?"

"The Sundance catalog thing. The, uh . . . Western Blanket!"

"Oh, yeah, sure." I fumble with the blade of the Waiter's Friend wine key. Nick the inside of my upper thigh, then put a cocktail napkin in my boxer briefs to sop up the blood. Sometimes there are episodes that leave things on a heavy, sort of deep note. Sad pop music plays over memorial clips, like that Green Day song did during the last *Seinfeld*. Sometimes they hit you pretty hard.

"Honey! It's on! What are you doing?"

Sometimes I wonder when a thing is a thing, or a them. Like, in the war we made *them* become *things*. (I mean, a guy is only a guy before you thunk him with an M203 grenade. Afterward? He's Ragú. Ragú is what we called it, what was left of it. Of them. So, like, he was a *them*, and then he was a *thing*. A Ragú.) Shea and I try to *make a them* out of a thing. A something out of nothing. Which we did, one time, just after the war. But the baby wouldn't stick inside her—for lack of a better term. So I suppose it went back from being a thing . . . to a them? I can't find a formula to describe it. Yet.

Sometimes I need to bleed just a slip. Eight, seven p.m. Central.

Gulp and gulp and gulp Nouveau and picture the friends

in the fountain. The fountain, the fountain. Azure marble
silver finish triple-Moen spontaneity. The friends jump in the
fountain. The actors don't really look like their own show
opening anymore. They're older in real life, with different
hairdos and everything. To some people it's probably kind of
weird that they stay the same age during the opening theme
song, when they all jump in a big fountain. But Shea and I
like it. We were their age when they started jumping in, so
it's kind of neat, you know, dreaming about being just out of
college, right when *they* were just out of college. And every
week, this fountain sort of kicks us into history. And there's
this stereo that Shea got me from Restoration. It's a brown
resin-plastic, fifties-style radio but with a CD player in it.

The friends always go to commercial after the fountain
opening, so a touch-up of wine to get past the break. I ask
Shea if we'd run out of body parts to compliment. She says
no way.

"Here's the Western Blanket, babe," I say, and drape it
across her small feet.

"It's actually a throw."

Oh. "Man, I love that radio," I say.

"Me too. It's dineresque. Oh, okay, I've got one."

"Where?"

"Sit down and lift up your shirt." I do, and she pokes me
near my left kidney. "That one. That inky bubble of mole. It's
gross, by the way."

"Haven't you already said that one?"

"Of course not," she says. "Wait. Maybe it's the one you
keep scratching off, dummy. So yes. But no. It's new—you
know? I don't know, check this out." She snatches the Resto-

ration catalog from this bamboo-looking magazine holder we got at Pier 1. "I really want this chair. Listen." She puts her hand on my forearm and begins reading. "A happy marriage of club chair and wingback produced these seats of compelling comfort and superlative style . . . Studs Terkel populism meets Dorothy Parker wit. Our La Porte Pressback Chair is built in the USA with a kiln-dried, double-doweled hardwood frame, high, rolled arms, and an angled wingback that promotes lounging, long talks, literary escapism, and languorous naps. Clad in luscious café velvet and accented with nailhead trim . . ."

"What the hell does all that mean? Who's Studs Turkey?"

We laugh ourselves to pieces. "I don't know," she says. "But look at that chair. Pretty cool, huh?"

Melt into photo, the crisp setup: (a) is the chair, (b) is the dual map lighted globe, (c) the leather archival photo albums, (d) antiqued bronze magnifying glass, (e) and (f) the black cherry bookcase AND credenza. And, and it's all quite intelligent. And I do like whatever that long literary talks thing.

"Well, maybe we could," I say.

She beams and starts to squeeze me, then, "Shhh. It's back on."

At the start of the season, Ross said Rachel's name while taking wedding vows with Emily. He tried to explain it away. Said they all live together as friends, etc. Shea and I agreed that the stupid foreign Emily character wasn't going anywhere, and sure enough it got done.

"Are we taping?" she whispers. "Yeah," I say. We have taped almost all of the *Friends* episodes, which is a lot. Tapes and tapes and tapes, and I'm toying with the idea of buying a DVD burner at Sharper, so we can melt them down to a decent size. It took us all last Labor Day weekend to catalog episodes. It was a blast, though. Wine and wine and wine and wine, though no Beaujolais, all fountain.

Beer commercial. "Shea, do you want to skip *Jessie* and just watch an old *Seinfeld* tape before *Frasier* comes on?"

"Are we gonna eat anything?"

"Sure. What do you feel like?"

"I don't know. What do you feel like?"

"Mmm . . . not sure. Oh, it's almost back on."

We both think Ross will marry Rachel. Shea thinks that Joey will marry Phoebe. Feebee. "What an awesome job," Shea says, when Monica talks about being a chef.

"Maybe. But I guarantee you she'll be a mom soon. And nothing's more important than that." I say this and then I don't know why I say it, because it's so goddamn hurtful.

Shea looks down at her chest.

"Sorry, sorry," I say. "Really. Need a splash, babe?" "Sure." "Hungry?" "Um, not yet, maybe. Hurry, you'll miss something."

People can be high-art or dismissive and snobby, but there's no getting around the fact that entertainment can be fun. I mean, holy mack, not only did Joey just remember getting a turkey stuck on his head, but Phoebe remembered a bad Thanksgiving from a *past life*. And get this: Monica just remembered the Thanksgiving when she actually cut off Chandler's little toe! (Jesus Christ, she was fat during the flashback. And Rachel had such a big ugly nose.) Shea and I hold hands, we smile, we have a drink of wine and laugh our eyes wet. We can talk to each other if things get bad enough.

Shea's thick-socked feet are burrowed into the folds of fine Anthropologie Cotswold leather. The waft of her delicate Aveda hair billows up from my lap. It's addictive. She looks up at me during the commercials and we talk about stuff we like. Sometimes she doesn't look up, and maybe there's stuff we like on the commercials, which is fine because we're warm. In the show there are no cysts on anyone's ovaries. No scarring no blockage no residue of thing. Here, flutamide takes care of her extra hair growth—which never bothered me in the first place. Shea is incredibly clever and funny. She points out that during all of the Bud Light commercials, there's a three-part comedy blueprint: Quirky Scenario, then Humiliating Explanation, and then, after the "talking part" where they espouse Bud Light in a sentence, and more importantly when you've become convinced that the story couldn't get any funnier— bam!—they hit you with Part Three: an instant, knockout joke to end the commercial.

I'm a number-pattern guy. I never thought about that story structure until she noticed it. But she's dead-on. That's the way they all play out. *Friends* is wrapping. One quick knock-out after the last commercial, then the preview of the next episode. I'm thinking maybe Wolfgang Puck. I don't know.

"Wolfgang Puck?" I ask.

"Okay," Shea says.

"Skipping *Jessie*?"

"I don't care, you decide."

"Microwave or oven?" "Microwave—oven takes too long." "Yeah." "Honey, will you grab your card so we can order the literature chair at the break?" "You sure? I mean . . ." "We'll get the miles." "That make you happy?" "Yes!"

She loves me, she really does. I love her, really do. We love each other. Truly. Honestly. More than most. I'll bet our lives on that.

"I love you," I say.

"I love you back," she says. And we both know it's not television.

And my god, fat Monica cut off Chandler's toe at their Thanksgiving, only instead of sending the detached digit to the hospital to be sewn back on, she mistakenly sent a baby carrot that had fallen on the floor beside it! I'll pop in a pizza but hold off on the tape until the local news comes on. "Let's give *Jessie* another chance?" "Okay." "The chair comes to $2,304.50, including ship." "Let's see, 2-3-0-4-5. You know, February 30 is almost like saying March 2." "You're cheating!" she shrieks. "Feb. 30 doesn't exist!" "I know, babe," I say, "But that's how it came to me. February 30, 1945. So, anyway, whose birthday?" "What?" "Come on. Work with me, silly. Who's birthday is March 2, 1945?" "My mother!"

Give *Jessie* another try and wine, and then *Frasier*. Slice off a toe like a bloody baby carrot. I can hear the wet knife. Can feel the wet knife. Jesus, I still have to check the email. Amazing how consuming the Internet's becoming. The chair is 5-4-3-2 then 0, missing 1. Just like Shea and I. March 2 is the day that Gulf War combat formally ended. Took 100 hours, on a 24-hour news cycle. Anyway, I'll log to email after *Frasier*, at the start of the *Seinfeld* tape. It's the one where Jerry dates a woman called "Man Hands" anyway, so I know how it starts.

Pickle

SYCORAX? TODAY?

Yes, even today, my brother plays a song featuring Syco-rax, an eerie, operatic soprano, which is why it's so difficult to be around him and Janine. As the clarinet snakes from the Wi-Fi jukebox, the few forlorn men at the bar peer up from their drinks. With the rise of the orchestral chorus they sigh, or pick at scabrous ears and necks, then resume a silent perturbation.

And I tell you there is nothing like chasing your father's funeral in a drop-ceiling honky-tonk, midday in Nashville, alongside agitated siblings and exit-ramp panhandlers . . . listening to German opera.

Danny walks back from the jukebox barking like Hitler. "*Brenne Laterne! Nahe und ferne dammere auf!*" I'm so tired of these roles. I only want to focus on what's happening here, to try and salvage something between the three of us. I love these people. Dad is dead.

"I recall this ditty," our sister, Janine, says, the strings and soprano wailing. She turns to Danny. "Dad playin' all that

Teutonic hostile stuff while y'all worked out in the garage, right?"

"Wagner," he says. "Spohr, and whatever. I hear it every time I exercise."

"Guys?" I ask. "Please?"

She rolls her eyes. Danny's jaw flexes.

Okay, I get it. I'll grant that Colonel Dad was a little freaky with the competition stuff, a bit too Bill Kilgore from *Apocalypse Now*. But it's not supposed to be like this today. Not between us.

"You know," I say to Danny, "I was so jealous of that. I always wished you guys would ask me to join you on the weight bench."

Danny nods, looks away.

Considering my brother's starched broadcloth shirt, and his lust to both embody *and* destroy convention, I can't help but mumble, "That painful to win so many trophies, Danny? Life so bad out in chichi Belle Meade?"

Janine turns to me. "What'd you say, baby? Wait. Don't answer, I don't wanna know." She wags the empty pretzel bowl at the bartender and starts to giggle. "Oh, god, do y'all remember the Chex Mix thing?" Her eyes dart to Danny and she covers her mouth, as if to take the question back. "Danny, sorry. Just slipped out."

"Jesus, sis, no worries," he says. "That was like thirty years ago!"

"Still," she says. "I can't believe he made you eat Chex Mix, every meal for a week, after *I* dropped a bowl of it into the furnace return. I swear, Dad making us suffer for each other's mistakes was, like, evil genius."

"Nah," Danny says. "It was just an old Basic Training trick. They were mostly just old Basic Training tricks brought home."

I look to the muted television above. *Spies Like Us* is on. Chevy Chase and Dan Aykroyd. I have seen this movie a hundred times in my forty-two years. Despite our father's having been the self-proclaimed "Baddest Lurp to Ever Sling a CAR-15" in Vietnam, it is this film, alongside *The Hunt for Red October*, that bookends my understanding of the Cold War.

"Frank's the reason," Janine tells me. "You act like nobody's to blame, Bobby. Like we should just be sad. But dead or no, Frank's still responsible for all our crap."

"Frank" means our father; this "crap" means her marriages.

She continues, "Somehow, I thought it would stop today. Visualized, you know, the three of us holding on to each other, like, letting go? But it didn't. It won't."

On the television, Chevy Chase performs his patented physical and facial comedy.

Janine is hung up on the moms that blotted her childhood. She chooses to forget that growing up we watched *Caddyshack* like fifty times, nuzzled up on a pillow pile on the floor in the den, everybody calling out the zingers, Dad impersonating Rodney Dangerfield, Danny steamrolling the heck out of Janine and me . . . all of us laughing our faces off.

"I remember when I got my first period . . ." she says.

I've heard her stories so many times.

". . . and Dad told creepy Uncle Pete."

Dad had to hear them too, whenever we all got together.

"I mean, *Uncle-friggin'-Pete*, for chrissake! You believe that? Like, he wasn't even our uncle! He was a retired Drill

Sergeant of female troops. Whose insistence was on observation and reprimand."

The past is a rerun, Janine. We must try and fast forward.

"I showered in my underwear for, like, a year."

Tell it to your new shrink. Or to Ellen, or Judge Judy.

Danny leans in to her, says, "I know, sis, I know." His right hand rattles the keys in his suit pants, while the left lovingly pats Janine's back. He whispers something in her ear, and she shakes her head, mouthing, It's okay, I'm all right. Danny then orders an Amstel, and marches it into the bathroom.

I take a deep, calm breath. "Dad's *dead*, Janine. We need to find something."

"You're lucky," she answers, her lousy breath on my face. "Know what I thought about today, Bobby? I mean, baby?"

"Shhh. I'm right here, sis. What?"

She leans in, whispers, "Sometimes I'm glad. Sometimes I'm *jealous* that Pickle died."

This is unacceptable. With her mention of our baby sister I can't help the thought of slapping Janine. I grind my teeth, then turn back to the television. Try to conjure something joyful.

Janine and I learned to ride a bike together, out at Percy Warner Park. The sunshine was spectacular, was white and blue and everywhere—only not in your eyes. White-blue sky, and she had white plastic tassels on her handlebars and a pink frame with periwinkle flowers on the white chain guard. I had a red, chromey Schwinn. And Dad and Danny took us to the top of this small grassy hillock and had us mount our bikes, side by side. The two of them held us upright, and kept telling us to calm down, to trust them, and that we didn't need any pansy training wheels. They then counted down together, Three-two-one—push!

Rushing down that slope, gravity took care of balance, and gave Janine and me confidence as we pedaled through the free fall. By the time we hit the bottom of the hill we knew how to ride. We pedaled out and into the open field, intuitively peeling off into separate circles, me to the left and Janine to the right, our tires matting down an infinity sign in the grass, in and out of each other's vision as Dad and Danny cheered from above. I can't remember who collapsed first, but at some point Janine and I simply stopped pedaling, slowed, and finally flopped with our bikes into the thick grass. (We didn't know how to brake!) Dad and Danny clapped as they lumbered down the hill to hug us.

"Come on, sis," I say now, wishing Dad hadn't been too cheap to buy a video camera. Evidence of that bike ride, of the good times, would've fixed all of us. As is, it's as if her memory has crushed out the love.

"Don't 'Come on' me," she says. "You don't know what it was like to be a girl in a military dictatorship."

My barstool scrapes the linoleum as I get up to go find my brother.

THE men's room is white-tiled and pungent. Danny urinates while glugging the Amstel, gently rocking back and forth.

"Can I talk to you, Danny?"

He doesn't answer, but only wobbles, back, forth, his

Armani belt clattering. He suckles the bottle, nipple-like, his piss traversing the mouth of the urinal.

"Danny?"

"Mmm," he grunts, peering sideways at me. His eyes are those of a cow trapped in a railcar. He won't take the bottle from his lips to speak. He can't.

"DANNY?"

He gurgles, pees, grunts—but won't stop. The way he rocks brings to mind a show I watched about Hasidic Jews praying at that Wall.

"You're *off*, man," I say, and then wash my hands and stare at the mirror.

WIFE after wife had nice bits to say about Dad at the memorial. Wife after wife, all women whom I'd only caught wisps of, being the baby and all, got up and noted their remembrances.

A) Danny's mom, Marie, noted that Dad "was so dedicated to his work." She has that raspy Memphis drawl.
B) "I remember when he surprised me with our dream house," said Janine's mom, Betsy, from beneath a veil of fly-screen lace.
C) Elaine—my birth mom—said, "I don't think I found Frank's heart, until little Pickle died."

I don't suppose I knew anything until little Pickle died. I was four and a half, and *she* had been the baby. Incredible: She would grab my thumb all the time, just grasp my thumb with her tidbit fingers. Danny would laugh at this and call me Fonzie, and I'd say, "Ayyyy." Everywhere we went people would swoon and tickle her, down in her stroller.

After the memorial, Elaine (C) came over to chat with me. "Hope I didn't disappoint you there, kiddo," she said, her smile now hatched by the drag of a million cigarettes.

"I'm not sure I follow," I answered. "I thought you were great."

"Oh, you know. The 'not finding Frank's heart' comment? Guess I got caught up in the chance at one last dig."

We stared at each other. "Oh!" I said. "'Heartless Frank!' Got it. No, no problem, Elaine. This is a hard day for everybody."

"Huh." She squinted, and briefly cocked her head. "Anyway, you look good, Bobby. You good?"

"I think so."

"Good," she said. "See you graveside."

I smiled as Elaine then seeped back into the *Land of the Lost*, her heels clicking the funeral home marble. This was, and is, just fine. I'm at peace with our relationship being not so very. From what I hear, over and over, Danny and Janine didn't give great ratings to the various women who dabbled in their childhoods.

MY list: Phoebe Cates in *Fast Times at Ridgemont High*. Both Jo and Blair in *The Facts of Life*. Wonder Woman. Chubby Tiffany-Amber Thiessen—with a secondary nod to the rest of the girls on the original *Beverly Hills, 90210*. Annie Hall. Vanna White. Showtime or Cinemax after ten p.m. in the old days. Nerdy Velma from *Scooby-Doo*. Audrey Hepburn. The woman from *Butch Cassidy and the Sundance Kid*. The vast majority of Eastern European female tennis players. Nicole Eggert, circa *Charles in Charge*, no later. Mrs. Huxtable on *Cosby*. Girl #3 in the "Urban Rebounder" infomercial. Madeleine Stowe, Ellen DeGeneres. Jaclyn Smith in *Charlie's Angels*. Daisy Duke. Vanessa Williams. Both Barbarella and Hanoi Jane. The gal from *Footloose* (back then, not now, not the goddamned remake). Susan Sarandon. Christina Ricci. Bette Davis. Jenna Bush. Never Katie Couric, sorry. Always—I mean any hour of any day—both Pam and Sissy from *Urban Cowboy*.

DANNY says he has to make a call. He pulls his BlackBerry out, but also walks to an old phone booth at the end of the bar. Janine orders another whiskey sour, then explains that she has no control over the "testing" of her current husband, Jeremy.

"It started out solid," she says. "Like the rest."

"Janine," I respond. "You've got to let—"

"I really loved him. You know I did, right?"

"You're too—"

"I think I still do. Plus, the twins." She grips her new drink. "The twins helped for a while."

Help or no, regardless, now, she's fallen back into the same old cycle. She sleeps around, religiously, throwing the litter of her liaisons in Jeremy's face, straight lie to sext to the Plan B boxes in the bathroom trash can, if only for the very necessary reason of making him prove how much he loves her.

Prove that he would never leave her, never screw around or keep secrets.

"Funny thing is," she says, "Jeremy's the only one that's hung in there!" Her laugh sounds like a metal rake on asphalt. "I almost hate him for being so wonderful to me!"

"That's because you're an ass, Janine. Period!" I can't help but yell at her. Her negativity is just too much.

"An ass? An *ass*, Bobby?" She wipes her eyes with her fingertips. "What do you know about anything?"

"I know that some of us need to just get over it."

"Over it?" she asks. "You were never *under* it, sweetheart. You never even got near it." She pauses for a moment, then. "Dammit, Bobby! I . . . I *prayed* to that man for guidance."

"Maybe if you hadn't—"

"In high school, I *prayed* to Dad to help me. To save me from myself. All I ever got back was, 'Janine, go help your mother.' Which was hilarious, since my 'mother' at that time was Huong Hiêú. She was twenty-two!"

"So he was a jerk sometimes," I say, quashing the impulse to yell out, *Order up!* our joke about the fact that Dad ordered Huong Hiêú from a catalog.

"A *jerk*?" she mocks loudly. "Dad made Huong Hiêú tutor me in wifedom, Bobby. She had me stroke the veggies before stir-frying them, then whipped me with kitchenware if I complained." She glares at me. "A *jerk*, Bobby?"

Order up! is also what Dad would yell to Huong Hiêú when he was hungry.

"Okay, okay." I hold up my hand up to stop her. "Gotcha. Bad word choice. But how could I not get it, Janine? Where do you think I was? We lived in the same house."

"I have no idea where you were," she says. "The only time I ever saw you cry was when he tried to turn off your ABC *Afterschool Special*."

At the other end of the bar, Danny hangs up both phones—cell in right ear, pay phone in left—and bolts back over. He asks what's going on, and then he and Janine have another moment where they gaze into each other's eyes and, as always, share some exclusive understanding. Woe. I look to the television.

A few minutes later, Danny admits that Dad bought him a hooker when he was in high school. Janine gasps and Danny swears it's true, explaining that it happened after he lost at state, junior year. He says Dad told him his cock was too big for his jock, and then dragged him down to some Asian joint on Nolensville Road. Janine's face gets long and slick and pouty, and she says, Oh, Danny, I'm sorry, because she's the one person who's never seen any of the nine million shows where Coming of Age is something a man can share with his son.

"Yeah, it was terrible, sort of," he says. "But maybe not—I don't know. Anyway, the point is that it was a onetime deal. Dad never counted on how much it would cost!"

At this, the three of us laugh until we can't breathe. I finally yell out, "Order up!" and we fall into hysteria, remembering Dad's international calls to Huong Hiêú's mail-order bride company, demanding a refund of his six thousand USD.

"The best part was that the company didn't understand his Vietnamese!" Janine exclaims.

"He stomped around like an infant, spewing babble,"

Danny howls. "Trying to reclaim authority over the country that made him impotent!"

Now this is real-deal joy.

Minutes later, Danny catches his breath. "What about you, pal?" he asks me. "Gotta girlfriend?"

Part of me wants to make up a tale about being cheated on, or a dead lover or something. Instead, I just try to keep smiling. "No. Not really."

I couldn't do much at the service, save mutter a few words about Dad being a cross between Mike Brady and the Great Santini. Nobody listened. At the national military cemetery north of town, the lawn and gravestones are so precise, so wonderfully green and white. We were surrounded by soldiers and guns. A flag was folded like a paper football and passed our way. (Who ended up with it? Betsy?) As I spoke, looking out at the teethlike rows of Union and Confederate and Other, the 4,131 Unknowns, Danny fingered his Black-Berry. Janine slunk away for a cig.

Throughout the service I pictured soap-opera funerals. How the distraught launch themselves about the grave, beating their fists on the coffin, their tears streaking its glassy, lacquered wood. At one point I even looked for the controversial former lover, in sunglasses on the fringe of the cemetery, ducking behind weathered stone arches at the gate. But none of that happened, which was disappointing. In fact, the absence of my own tears made me feel so guilty I considered seeking out another funeral altogether—until "Ashes to ashes." At that point I was hit with loss. Indeed, a sense of loss, for a moment, as those lines spilled over Dad and into the cool earth below.

IT took a while to really get it down pat. You don't just start off perfectly fucking a television. You start off, of course, masturbating in front of it. Everyone does. And it's good. Really good. And then things progress, and you get the idea. You get up off the couch, walk over, grapple the sides of the console and start humping at the unit, which is of course silly. (Surely, you look like a happy dumb dog forcing its instinctual hips into nothing.) Only, it's not as good as it should be. So you practice and prod, and grumble and bumble, and then buy a bigger television; surround sound; recordable, full-throttle digital satellite; movie subscriptions, On Demand, etc. Then you purchase a hypo-allergenic latex "Pocket Snatch"—which sort of works, as you squeeze into it with one hand, the other caressing the console of the boob tube, the remote in immediate vicinity.

But really, that sort of *doesn't* work either. It's too mechanical. What works completely, you discover, after years of disappointment, is when you plant the head of a life-sized, gel-enhanced sex goddess (kind of like an X-rated CPR dummy with the most realistic pubic hair you ever dreamed of, plus a surprisingly tight synthetic anus) under a *smaller* television set which has been leaned back against the wall at a forty-five-degree angle—and then mount the protruding body while gazing into the eyes of the screen.

This works because you can then watch a skin flick, or celebrity game show, or nightly news or family drama or awards ceremony or women's tennis match or soap opera or beer commercial or reality show, or whatever . . . a rerun, a premiere . . . and you can literally take it into your arms and fuck the guts out of it. Or make love. Or cuddle. Or caress. Or confess, or cry. Whichever you prefer.

What's transcendent is that it fucks *you*, confesses to you, accepts you, admires you, fantasizes with you, evolves with you, shares with you, adjusts with you, understands you. Loves you back. Unconditionally, unconditionally, unconditionally.

Until they come up with a woman who has a console for a head, I fear that's the best I can do to give love.

WHEN Janine goes outside to smoke, Danny starts confessing. "I can't stop multitasking, Bobby. I can't control, and it's getting worse and worse and . . . I'm worried that Beth is going to leave me."

His liquor-laced whispers convey such helplessness; it's as if he doesn't understand himself. He notes that, as I've seen, he must replace his urine with fluid intake the instant he evacuates—as if he never over-internalized Dad's demands to dominate both offense and defense, "both sides of the goddamn ball." Danny says that for whatever reason, he can't make a bowel movement without brushing his teeth—as if Dad never criticized his ROTC and Reserve commitment, or, hell, even his *war*, as being "not nearly tight enough." He swallows hard, says, "Bobby? For chrissakes, Bobby, I can't even make love to Beth unless I've got one eye on the *Wall Street Journal*"—as if Dad didn't call him a faggot after he was promoted to regional vice president with B of A.

This is so one-segment-of-*Dr.-Phil* recognizable. I'm about to suggest that he try cheating with a flat-screen, when Janine staggers back in, her silhouette breaking up the bar-door sunlight.

WE all shifted when Pickle died. Little Pickle-face, not quite three years old. She was the baby, and was Dad's chance at redemptive fatherhood. The nearly navy-blue eyes that meant to serve as peacemakers, as liaisons, between Dad and Danny and Janine and me, and which would at last make us a real live, functional family.

Eighteen months my younger sister, her life defined by the Monroe Carell Children's Hospital at Vandy. She never had a chance to contemplate heaven or hell or the Easter Bunny. Yet somehow, as I look around at all of us, maybe it's not so bad after all: little Pickle's death.

Shhh.

Maybe, as I think about Janine—thirteen and already destroying her body—I did get off easy. Maybe, when I think about Frank's incessant degradation of Danny, I got lucky as hell.

Yeah, maybe, just like Janine (but for different reasons), I'm glad Pickle died. Maybe the black circles under her eyelids and her hairless little head, the paper ducks taped to the ward wall, were worth it—just to again become the baby of the household. To escape my father, who after Pickle's death just gave up on all of it: his wives, his children, his military career. Who turned me over to a brightly pixelated babysitter.

Maybe, just maybe, I was lucky to be parented by the screen. To sit for hours alone, to always look for Pickle, always always always, and to find shards of her on *Sesame Street* and *The Cosby Show* and *Growing Pains* and *Laff-A-Lympics* and . . . To find him there as well: Good Ole Dad. Or, rather, Good New Dads. Flawless and nonthreatening, a thousand different men who taught me how to live. Loving me, forgiving my faults. Providing the practical wrap-ups that Janine and Danny never knew.

Janine walks back in from her smoke and plops down on the barstool.

"Sorry, Bobby," she says. "It's just a weird, awful day and all."

"No," I say. "I'm the one who's sorry, sis." I picture the deepest hug I've ever watched, and try my best to give her one that eclipses it.

Because yeah, maybe.

Wall

so,

it used to be that night after night I'd lie dead awake, staring at the street-lit silhouette of lace drape on bedroom wall. Hours of halogen, the silence broken only by the report of low-caliber gunshot on the streets, or by the smashing of bottles in the alley below. Used to be heart arrhythmic, in the gut of anxiety, aphasia, dysthymia, and back-of-throat-scrape reflux. I was home. Honorably discharged. I had transitioned from CHU barracks to a series of moves, south then north, and to this matchbox apartment in the city. A chair and plank of desk. To cracked, cream and cornflower linoleum of kitchenette adjoined to shower-stall bathroom. To gilt-frame picture from before the war. Pens with clotted ink. Fatty rinds trimmed from markdown cutlets graying in the drain-catch. Dress greens with combat ribbons in back of closet, moth cakes in pocket. To tight on sour bourbon, hand-sweeping crumbs and dust from the corners while bent down to recover some dropped object. A bottle top. Fork.

To the questions: *Wasn't there another way? Couldn't I have chosen not to—? But Father, can't you understand that—? Chaplain, can you—? Could you—?*

No, nobody could. The facts were only fork and bottle top; were a glass and a glass, and dips of shallow sleep, propped up on folded foam pillows to curb the climbing flux. Glances at the red digits of the alarm clock. At the wall stamped with silhouette of lace drape. Streetlight halogen. Ever awake.

so,

used to be nights and nights, liminal, unending, until one night I heard something new, through the wall. I shot awake. *What was that?* Heart pound. *A knock? Who's there? Hello?* I reached for my weapon and . . .

No, it's nothing, I thought. *Just the snag of apnea.* It was nothing. *Now settle in. Settle down.*

I de-cocked the MK, and forced myself back to nourishing thoughts of Supposed-To-Be. (This time, I imagined that instead of enlisting, I'd gone into medical sales, achieving both base salary and commission.) Back to balmy summer, Birmingham, Alabama, and to her premature crow's-feet and gold-flecked hazel eyes; to a Toyota Tacoma, graphite-black, certified pre-owned; to wood-fenced yard to mow on Sunday; to thinking of getting pregnant, and fifteen-year fixed rate; periodic nightlife of old fraternity buddy in town, and let's try the new Japanese restaurant near the mall; to grocery store valentine for her, with love, true love, never left you love, fill me up love, spaniel puppy at Christmas, better than yesterday love; in-laws and the bottles of twist-off Merlot they offer; to she and I drive down to the Gulf for the three-day weekend, or maybe San Fran on Southwest for four; my turn to sweep the pubes off of the potpourri scent-filled, one-out-of-two-and-a-half-bathroom tile floors; to the shouts and the fights, and to the hours curled up watching sitcoms; to joke emails at work, and work emails at home, and . . .

To your toothy, stuttered laugh so lovely. Let's please just grow old.

To can't sleep. So very old. *Was that a knock?*

Indeed. A knock. And that's when I began to hear her, through the wall.

I listened to the rip of the packing tape from her boxes, and to the stacking of plates in the cubbies over the sink. I heard her pause to consider her trinkets. Heard her reprimand herself when she dropped something sentimental.

(By accent she is British. Lilting. But broken.)

Side-by-side in our crumbling walk-ups, I knew that the streetlight hit her bedroom wall. Understood the curl of her linoleum. I listened and heard a thousand lovers, a million, hourly wage jobs. City to town, spiraling farther away from home.

She did a lot of late-night, pan-crash cooking. Sang Mozart libretti. I believe there were quick raps on the wall when I snored too loud, or got too drunk. When she was trying to read, or just wondering how she'd gone wrong back in soggy old England. At times, I made out hints of her phone calls: —*ther, I can't believe you'd say that when you know very well he never cared for me,* or *I don't have it right now,* and I listened to her halfhearted prayers. I fell mad for her vocal tone, which tingled my neck muscles, tickled my cochlea. After hearing her leave, I'd sneak into the hallway and inhale her traces.

AND,

over the weeks, we grew. As if on orders, I made things proper for her. I bought bottled water and lilac-scented candles; some British cookies, called McVitie's, and double bergamot tea. Marmalade. At the library, I studied: map room to Internet kiosk, *Mirror* and *Sun* to *BBC News*. *Così fan tutte* in the A/V extension. I found out my Birmingham was named after hers.

I also worried about inadequacies. *My god, I must try to stop drowsing into terror, must try to stop drinking, try to smile— well, maybe not smile, but just not frown, not scowl, nor curse so loud . . . nor do anything vulgar in the bedroom or she'll hear me and She's All I've Got* type of thoughts, defined and redefined themselves.

Once in a while she'd fall silent for hours, as if she'd moved on. I still don't know why. I don't know. To provoke a response I would pace around talking loudly to myself, clanking glasses and dropping things. Would pore over a Tupperware full of photographs and letters from all those stations left behind. Places raped by battle. People or actions that will never let me be. Choices that never forgive.

I blurted the old rants, cursed the old beliefs, felt so stupidly old. Put on my moth-eaten dress greens, got into bed and stared at my wall and lace drape, a whiskey glass on my belly, and . . .

Wait. What was that?

Somehow, always, she'd be there after all, a hummingbird's worth of flutter through the partition. Listening!

THEN,

there was a visitor. A man.

As he cleared his tar-thick throat I realized he'd been there before—perhaps all along. To counter his grunts, I cleaned the shower with steel wool and bleach, the scalding water burning me, blistering my hands and forearms. It was not enough. Desperate to camouflage his moans, I started to experiment with distraction, with delusion or pain. Ultimately, I found that adding a spoonful of Ajax to my whiskey provided hours of constriction, my body writhing as the sweat and saliva worked to evacuate the poison.

Nothing can overpower *that.*

He insulted her cooking—though he never cooked. So I began to prepare meals, as a partner should. Pasta carbonara, with fresh Reggiano, ground pepper, finely chopped pancetta, two farm eggs—a dish I perfected while home-nursing an elderly Lazian whose children had milked his pension until he passed. (I hated my complicity in their avarice, but such was the murky economy outside of Camp Darby, Livorno. Or outside of *any* American military base.) On Sunday mornings I whipped up two plates of Rednecks Benedict, poached eggs with brown gravy and bacon in lieu of Canadian ham and hollandaise; a heart-clogging spread I invented post-military, while working a family grill outside of Batesville, Mississippi. I thought maybe she'd get a kick out of that. (Or, hell, maybe she'd refuse but still appreciate a copy of the *Herald Tribune*, bought from the specialty market all the way downtown.) I bought wine instead of whiskey and allowed that I can cook veggie burgers and veggie-veggies—whatever she prefers. "We can go out, if you want," I offered the air. "Down to Brump's, to a booth of smoking or non-, no problem." To play billiards and flirt like candlelight, and bicker and laugh at the young, the brazen. Be young and brazen. *We could*, I thought, *we could we could* . . .

And this has been days and months, as measured by replications of red alarm clock digits, by the hum of streetlamp, and by listening. By at last fearing nothing: No man, No god, No fucking bomb, No death, No failure.

At last, with her, I am not a failure.

YESTERDAY,

I woke to her side of a phone argument. I got out of bed and bent close to our wall, caressing it until I could best hear her. The shouts made plain that she was fighting her second-tier, bullshit lover. He was no good for her, she said. She said that he was addicted to breaking her, to mending her, and then to breaking her again—but that there was someone else who understands.

Someone who will take me home, she said.

She moved so close as she stated this. I heard her breathe between phrases, maybe even smelled the tint of her salt. She told him that he is unable to trust or give, and that he's a slob, and that she's not some random fantasy. She explained that she loved hibiscus tea—did he know? Did he know that she is scared to death of the forest?

But that's not the point, she said. She told him that for once, for once in her goddamned life she wants someone who's not out to crucify, resurrect, or alienate her pain. Or her joy.

My god, I thought. *You're talking to me, aren't you?*

Yes. She was talking to me. Because we have been here so many, many times before. Battle to battle, slaughtering, staggering on.

But perhaps, I thought. *Perhaps we can finally just go home.*

Last night, I poured my whiskey into the sink, arranged my pillows on the floor, and then slept like a lamb against our wall. In the instant before drowsing, I heard her make her pallet there as well.

TODAY,

her door buzzer rang and rang. I'd slept through the night—slept late, in fact—and so I knew that she was already at work. I tried to ignore the interruption, but the caller held the button for a minute or more. After a brief pause, my own door buzzer rasped, and then a knock rattled my windowpanes.

Her lover, I thought. I unholstered the MK and placed it on the kitchen counter, ready to be done with him at last. Stared at the door, inhaled, and opened.

It was only the postman, sighing and rushed, holding a brown-papered parcel for her, from abroad. I signed for it and stepped into the hallway, and watched him stomp away.

Should I leave her a note? I wondered, my chin resting on the package. *Show up in person when I hear her return? Hand her the package and . . . Anyway, this is it, this is it!*

I paced the hallway like a nervous teen. Laughed at myself as I ducked back inside my apartment, and placed the package on my desk. *Settle in, shh. Maybe I'll just leave a card with my—*

I sat and stared at the parcel, my bare feet tapping the floor, my left hand trembling. Took in the scrawled handwriting of the address, and the sender's alien zip code of letters and numbers. I wondered who on earth still used twine to seal a box (and suspected it was her mother). *Maybe there's a photo inside, a fact. Perhaps I could peer. Could finally, finally see her.*

No. I stood up, and began to cook our meal, chopping fresh vegetables and peeling citrus and . . . and I turned on the radio, twisting station to station to find the opera, and . . . *My god, how am I to do this? A note? Perhaps a funny note or sketch on the brown paper? Yes. A smiling face in a doorframe, my name printed underneath. Or maybe nothing funny—just an invite to dinner. Or perhaps I could . . .*

No. I stopped, slid down onto the floor, my back against the cabinet and my legs straight out. Ordered myself to ignore things until my thoughts became clear. We had come so far for this. *But not too far? Just has to be right, that's all. Just right.* Yes. Let's say we open a restaurant, I thought. *The Bottle Top.* A tiny place, nothing fancy. Four or five tables, in one of those dusty storefronts down the block. Come to think of it, one of those spaces has been for lease since I moved here, so maybe we can work a good deal from the landlord. You and I will labor together, and gripe over the disjointed menu. Hibiscus tea. I'll clean, mostly, to keep you happy. We can use the mismatched plates of our apartment—it'll be quaint, you know? Carbonara. I can make this when you need nights off. Success will be difficult, I know, but how about we set a time frame? *Yes.* Set a one-year time frame where we both live in one tiny unit; tough it out in order to free up funds, to make this thing happen. I can already imagine the number of times we'll have to remind each other: *Remember, it's only for a year!* Ten months left, love. *Hang in there, babe.* Bottle of wine, here's to six more months. We can do it. Ninety days. We can, and we will, and

    No.

It took a minute to realize that I'd fallen asleep on the kitchen floor. It was dark out, the room smeared by shadow. My spine locked in pain from having been seated too long with my back against the cabinet. I stood up slowly, stretched. Listened.

She was home.

I snuck out into the hallway, and placed the package outside her door. Came back in and bolted the lock.

Ours can be no more than a silhouette of lace drape. We must risk nothing more than a wall.

so,
    with a little knock, good night.

We Come to Our Senses

THE BARS HAVING closed at midnight, we turned to guns. Within an hour, the back deck of Douglass and Willie's house became a killing field of empty Miller cans and Camel butts. And though we'd only shot one cockroach between the three of us, I'd taken it out hip-hop-style, pistol held sideways. No American sniper could top that shit.

At some point Willie went inside for a beer, then came back out shirtless. A Super 8 camera was tucked in the waistline of his jeans. He said he'd snagged the camera at Thrift City, where he'd gone to ditch his ex-wife's souvenir spoon collection. Douglass and I grabbed for it but he swatted us away. He said we couldn't waste a frame of film, then yanked it out and stuck the viewfinder to the port-wine'd half of his face. "Slaughter!" he directed, and Douglass stomped the deck with his roper boots, and roaches sprang from the gaps between the rotting lumber. I took aim and fired the pistol. Though the BB gun proved inaccurate, the hum of the camera motor was thrilling.

Being a film guy, I asked where was our shoot-'em-up

soundtrack? Where was Morricone when you needed a decent film score? They didn't get it.

"Sergio Leone?" I followed. Nada.

I'd started to whistle the theme from *The Good, the Bad and the Ugly* when Darla called, wondering when I'd be home. I cocked the cell phone away from my ear and said, Soon and I love you. I hoped that this was fair, but she was agitated—perhaps on account of her new meds, perhaps not. I tried to muffle the crack of another beer, but the rip of the aluminum set her off. Willie and Douglass shook their heads in judgment as I then indulged her lengthy grievance. They no longer had time for relationships, having decided to spend their post-divorce lives as born-again bachelors. Their ex-wives had both been cheaters, one a turned lesbian.

When I hung up, Willie announced that we were all going out to film a live-action horror movie, then aimed the camera at me for a response. I said, "Go for it, I've gotta go home." Douglass promptly called me pussyman (camera pans to him), and then stood up and asked me when was the last time anybody did anything worth a damn in this little town, like made a film or anything, and what did it say about me that I couldn't just take one night, one silly night off of playing by someone else's rules?

"Think about *that*," he said, the Super 8 fixed on him for effect.

I'd heard this speech every time we got drunk—only never on camera. I got yet another beer from the cooler and did think about it while they went in the kitchen to gather knives and other horror-flick props. Sitting alone on the deck, the Mississippi swelter lapping me like a dog tongue, I overhead them arguing about Douglass not drinking his Metamucil. Willie asked him why this was. Douglass didn't answer. "You can't even taste it in the water," Willie said, and asked if it was out of spite. No response. Finally, Willie threatened to stop doing their goddamn laundry if Douglass insisted on nurturing a spastic colon.

"That's enough!" Douglass barked in a hushed but commanding voice, reminding Willie that I was just outside and could hear them. Willie said he didn't care, and fell silent as if to sob.

I didn't care. It had taken me two years in Mississippi to make two friends. Two years of pining for the city and holding the move South against Darla. So no small, awkward quarrel would put me off of these guys. I needed them. No matter their addiction to camouflage, their fear of an unseen governmental force, or the way in which they echoed the gummy bickering of an elderly couple, I needed them. What's more, I thought, I *wanted* to need them. I wanted to keep shedding the things I held against this place before moving here, if only to find the complicated truth of Darla's Mississippi.

In any event, having decided that I would in fact stay out and make the horror film, I moved on to imagining Tyrone Power in the 1946 adaptation of *The Razor's Edge*: his struggle to resist social code, his mendicant odyssey in pursuit of true enlightenment.

I called Darla, and could hear *Law & Order* in the background.

"*Law & Order*, Jesus Christ," I said.

"Really?" she scoffed.

"Yeah, really. I mean, is this what it's come to with you?"

"Am I wrong to assume that you're shooting roaches with a couple of crypto-queer, misogynist rednecks?" she asked.

"Stereotyping them distracts from my point."

"Which is?"

Which is that back in the city, we watched films like fiends. We went to them throughout the week. We bought them in the discount bin at the grocery, or on the street. We went to festivals, to talks, we held screenings in our dinky apartment. We could hold entire conversations comprised of dialogue ripped from various movies, as reconfigured to fit any given topic.

We created a blog, a couple's movie-critic blog and website that had been featured in the city's weekly arts paper, and even mentioned in a few national industry trades. It got so many hits that theaters and script-consulting services bought banner ads. We'd even scheduled studio time and were going to film tiny episodes of our critical selves for public-access television. Our friends and their friends who knew us said it'd be amazing: our informed squabbling on camera. I built a stage-sized diorama that looked like an old television set, the frame a rich mahogany console with tweed beige speaker covers and clunky chrome knobs. We would do our thing inside this console-frame—only, our interior set would be painted black-and-white, and we'd be dressed and made-up in diverse shades of black and white. (Sitting at the oval oak table of our apartment, Darla and I batting around ideas, I got so excited about this that I suggested we review only *color* films, clips of which would be shown on a monitor between us, in our black-and-white interior . . . all meta-framed by the retro color television diorama, and of course the viewer's world, and she said that this would be too much, too clever and easy, and for a moment I thought of pushing my concept, really shoving it through her, before I realized she was right.)

Our set, our life together, was like a movie within a movie. I was bursting to build additional dioramic sets, to constantly change our frame. Theater set, drive-thru set, or iPhone set—we would always be inside something else, twice.

Darla never admitted it, but we both knew her talent was leagues ahead of my straight-man role. She was going to knock people out, playing up her drawl and being funny and intellectually savvy and herself.

But her infection went crazy, and her anxiety followed suit. So instead we moved South, to be close to her parents, to this bitsy Mississippi town where the bars close at midnight and are shut on Sunday and where they don't even have public access and where I never find a job and am constantly sweaty. The old, two-screen theater on the town square has been closed for years, and is rented out by a Southern Baptist start-up. (The marquee is sociopolitical precision: DIRECTIONS TO HEAVEN: TURN RIGHT AND GO STRAIGHT!) Our blog never changes but is still there. I visit it and read the dead past. Her parents go to great lengths to make us appear normal and vaguely class-appropriate for their tastes, reminding us that Mississippi is, as those in the right company say, "more a club than a state." They cosigned on a house we could never afford even if I had a job. We get cable and a tiny allowance, permitting Darla to wield a work narrative of nonprofit part-timing and progressive volunteerism, with an eye towards whatever state-run, arts-ed position she'll be nepotized into—and which she'll be great at.

Law & Order droning away, Darla asked me how old I was, then reminded me that her folks were driving up to take us to church the next morning. I love her so, but Christ, how much more sacrifice? Wasn't I *here* in Mississippi for her? Had I not left everything *for* her, my art and community and city and *identity*, tagging along as she loped home to privilege? Was it really so bad that I was going to stay out and *make* something?

"You know what, Dar?" I barked. "This is *Five Easy Pieces* and I am Rayette Dipesto, the waitress, and you are the rich-ass Jack Nicholson character who never feels the gut-sting of not always having everything, every single day of your life. But some of us were born without a net, baby!"

"Whatever, retard," she said, and hung up.

I looked into the backyard, at this old chrome dog bowl freckled in mud. Willie's dog, Slump, had died before I even moved to town. Yet his ghost hung around, care of fridge-photos and in doorway floor scar, and in gigs of sprawling video on Willie's phone. There was the anecdote about the time Slump managed to open the camping cooler, then ate thirty-two squares of Kraft Singles (with plastic wrap), drank a can of Miller Lite, and passed out. The tales of him retrieving live ducklings out of the pond in Town Park, or humping the service dog on the square on Veterans Day. I had come to know Slump as almost a nephew, a dead nephew dog, and I wondered sometimes if I needed a dog of my own, if owning another life would help Darla and me move forward, providing us a whole new history of love.

The boys and I piled into Douglass's old Bronco, then hit the road with sour mash. I took a drink, said, "Make no mistake, guys. I *adore* Darla." They had no reply. I then changed the topic to filmmaking: "You know, Larry Semon was from Mississippi. He was a big motion picture—"

"Ha!" Willie cut me off. "His name was *Semen*?"

"That would *so* suck," Douglass said, and the two of them cackled.

Had I been talking to Darla, or at least to *old* Darla, we would have worked up our shtick while discussing Larry Semon, the forgotten rival of Chaplin, the recipient of a $5,000-a-week studio salary in the 1920s, who became a fever drunk at the apex of his success and decided to make a slapstick version of *The Wizard of Oz*, in 1927 (twelve years before the one we all know), with Oliver Hardy as the Tin Man, and with drunk Semon's drunkard wife cast as Dorothy. A failure so enormous it decimated his career. Died in a California sanitarium, Larry Semon.

But old Darla was not here. The city was not here. The diorama set was not here. It seemed that my only markers of continued growth, of life, were Douglass and Willie, and the film we would make in the Mississippi night.

Douglass stopped off at this boarded-over Victorian shitheap, then got out and snuck around back. He and Willie buy old houses from poor blacks and use Mexicans to fix them up so they can fleece young whites. They started doing so when Douglass was still married to Gina, having bought their first project house care of her VA home loan benefits. Though he and Willie now do quite well, flipping houses all over town, they never update anything in their own home, out of disdain for their benefactress. "Don't owe Gina or nobody for nothin'," Douglass says, as if not spending the money he makes exempts his indebtedness to her.

As Willie and I waited, the engine cut and ticking, he confessed that he was worried sick about Douglass. Said he wished Douglass didn't have to act like such a stupid, stubborn man. I wasn't sure how to respond, so I didn't. Willie went silent and picked at his cuticles. A minute later Douglass walked back toward us, something big and dark cradled in his arms. He fumbled to open the Bronco's tailgate, then thunked it in the back.

The stench was a crucifixion of the sinuses. I vomited out the passenger's window, and began to regret the decision to anger my rich wife. Willie writhed and banged his head against the dashboard. Douglass was somehow unfazed; he laughed, and informed us that it was only a bloated dog carcass. A dead boxer, he said, which he'd found locked in the crawl space when first inspecting the Victorian, its body amid chewed Ziploc bags. He surmised that the dog had eaten whatever it was supposed to guard down there, meth or crack, then OD'd and baked in the heat.

We drove off with our heads flung doglike out the windows. A few minutes later, on a residential street, Douglass cut the headlights and rolled to a stop in front of Gina's house.

"This is gonna be horrorific," he whispered, then got out and went for the dead dog. Gas hissed out of the boxer when he picked it up, and a dark liquid ran down the front of his shirt. Douglass cursed God, demanded help. Willie said he had to hold the camera, then raised the Super 8 like a fist. I cursed God, then got out and grabbed the dog's back legs. The muscles were mush; it seemed as if the beast would crumble from the bone, like decent pork shoulder.

We snuck onto Gina's front porch heaving with nausea. The dead dog gassed out and made a slick smack when we dropped it. My phone vibrated in my pocket. I knew it was Darla.

Douglass whispered, "Okay, now ram a knife in it."

"Hell," I said. "I'm going home."

He started to argue when the front door flew open. There was Gina, holding us down with a modified twenty-gauge, and clad in olive-green panties and a tan muscle shirt, her dog tags swaying. She had black chevron tattoos on each sculpted deltoid, and she barked commands at us in both Arabic and English.

Douglass cried out for Jesus Christ and calm. From the car, Willie laughed and pointed the camera at us.

"A movie within a movie," I muttered, staring at the lens.

A legion of cops screeched onto the set. They clubbed us for many minutes and we were charged with alcoholic terrorism.

In the holding cell, Willie and Douglass bickered on as if they were back at home, sitting in twin recliners in front of their television. Across from them I was on my back, on a stainless steel bench, staring at the ceiling. I couldn't stop thinking about dogs. About Slump, and the dead boxer. I pictured the latter, frenzied on meth, smashing his head against whatever trapped him in the crawlspace. Smashing and smashing until his dog heart exploded. I could picture his final movements, so very slow in the heat, his last breath leaking out in a whistle.

"Or was it a *her*?" I asked aloud.

An hour or so later, Willie and Douglass ran out of gripe. In the silence, the jail toilet ran, and we may have even dozed. At some point I looked over and there was Darla, on the other side of the bars, wearing her sky-blue church dress.

"Hey, Dar," I said.

"Hey," she replied, her eyes raw from tears. "I'm bailing you out. But then we're done."

I begged forgiveness, mentioned Robert Duvall in *Tender Mercies*. Her mouth turned up a sad kind of smile. As I walked out behind her, fractured and stinking, Willie promised that next time he'd load film in the Super 8, now that we had an idea of what to expect.

D. Garcia Brings the War

HIGHWAY. GET TO drinking. Driving to the cemetery I get to drinking, hard. I look over at the passenger seat, and to Berea: hitchhiker, maiden, at our mercy. She is car-window-framed by tumbling gray clouds that still haven't decided if they'll break or not. I look at blond Berea and ask if she's heard of Petrarch. She asks back if he's like Bruno Mars. I say, Hell, no, Berea, then take a pull off the bourbon bottle and tell her that Petrarch was this Italian dude who wrote over two hundred sonnets to a woman named Laura. Wrote them over the course of twenty-something years. He was pure, you know. As was she: Laura.

Well, that's pretty great, Berea says, the Kentucky forest streaking by. Is this, like, a Mexican thing, D. Garcia? she asks.

I punch the gas as Pete butts in from the backseat, yapping that George Harrison and Eric Clapton each wrote songs expressing love to Clapton's wife, nicknamed Layla. Berea says she knows about Layla—the song anyway—and then

Pete corrects himself and notes that maybe it was Harrison's wife, but either way, it's romantic.

Jesus *fuck*, I say, we are not talking about a hippie rock star wife-swap, Pete. Like, Petrarch *didn't even know* Laura, man. He saw her like once, ONCE, from afar, and her purity drove him to throttle this sort of absolute unknown romance pain love to the extreme. I mean, she was married, had kids—was *off-market*. But Petrarch kept on loving, he kept on loving the very idea of her—while respecting her enough not to pressure her. His poems like a highway, his love a pure pilgrimage, a mission, a conquest, a Cause, a . . .

Laura! Laura! Laura! I howl. Bang the bottle on the dashboard, take a healthy pull and say, Hell, Pete, Petrarch sure as shit didn't have to put anything on the radio, or make a pop-culture spectacle out of love.

Berea coos this ethic. She squeezes my shoulder, smiles and caresses the back of my neck . . . but then turns back to fawn over Pete, too. In the rearview I see him roll his eyes at her, which prompts her to reach back between our seats and tickle him, which gets me crazy jealous—and to more of that bourbon. I swerve a little bit to scare her back up front. So then I'm drinking and thinking of Laura when Berea asks: Speaking of music, guys, do y'all have any Toby Wayne in the car? which almost makes me throw her farm-bred, hitchhike, downy white ass back onto the parkway, and which does make Pete respond, No way, Berea, because we totally hate that guy, and we hate pop-country crap in general, though . . .

You won't believe it, Pete continues, but D. Garcia's buddy, the guy we're staying with when we get to Nashville, wrote a song that megastar Toby Wayne recorded, at which point Berea freaks out and says, No way! twice, before asking, Which one? to which Pete responds, Jesus, I don't know, ask D. Garcia! to which Berea replies, D. Garcia, which one, oh, man, which song, which song?

And she's so beauteous and porcelain and maidenhead-clean when she begs. I plug another gluggeroo, then go ahead and answer, "Urban Cowgirl."

Well. Berea starts bouncing on the gray bucket seat, up and down, jiggling and spouting, Oh, my god, that's my favorite song of all time, ever, no way! No way! No Way! She begs me, Please, D. Garcia, you gotta take me to Nashville, I can't believe you know "Urban Cowgirl"!

And jesus christ if we're gonna be able to work this out. Stuck in this ride, her boobs bobbing like Cinemax, and Pete handing out Xanax, and I'm gonna pass y'all the bottle in a minute, but first *uno mas* for *moi*, and, No way, Berea, hell, no, we can't put on a pop-country station, no matter how much you sing and swoon. And hello, Hydrocodone; What's up, Weed?; and pass bottle, pass bottle, pass pass pass; snort snort glug snort pass pass snort . . .

and those car cabin sloppy hours melt into the dark, smeary sky . . . the same sky that pressed down during the torrential rains in the desert . . . the slate-gray sky and the slop nobody told us about while we trained on trucks at Leonard Wood, or before deployment from Bragg all those years and miles ago. They gave us no briefing of rain, no training for the mucosal, thrushy slop, the slop that turned the void in on the gut of the land itself, and into something darker. Something thick and unrelenting in our clothes, in our boots, in the slathered folds of our oily skin, yes,

we now slip like that, like truck tires in slop sand, like tires burdened by forty-ton rigs, slugging for traction or meaning, for anything beyond the Cause. Oh the Cause, my god Laura how it trudges over love

until finally, we reach the forlorn little cemetery, in the woods at the end of some cracked country road. A mist slicks us as we trip out of the car. The wet wind shakes the web of naked tree branches that spurt driblets of spring buds like green acne. We are stumbling in Kentucky, sticky-moist and the bottle down to a thin finger of bourbon, having detoured a hell of a ways from Nashville on Berea's behalf. Unknown Berea, our investment in pure. She is our belief that the miles and the years and the love in the books will be redeemed. That the songs and the flags will be replenished, if we can just move past ourselves, past our infidel past, and back to the Cause, and,

Berea says she doesn't know where her mom's grave is. She wanders the cemetery all wobble-legged drunk and ungrateful; So sue me, she says, you didn't have to bring me here, Garcia. All I ever did was ask.

Pete gets his guitar out of the trunk, takes a piss on some chrysanthemums, props up against a gravestone and starts fingerpicking country blues.

The sharp wind whips Berea's print dress up her thighs. She staggers by headstones and reads the names aloud. I call them back to her in slur until at last we locate her mother: a large slick gray block atop a grainy cement base.

My mom died too, I say.

My mom died, Berea says.

My mom died longer ago, I say.

This isn't about your mom, Berea slurs. It's not about YOU!

I slap her white-pink face. I don't think I mean to; I haven't slapped a maiden before. But I slap her and start to apologize, and then don't. Can't. Her blue eyes idle in momentary disbelief before she yanks the bottle from my hand and drains it, then stomps over and smashes it against some soul now known only as Taken from Us. I turn to Pete, who looks elsewhere while trying to pluck some stupid riff, and I yell, Fuck you, Pete, you recessive runt, you'll never take a woman to protect. Berea storms into my face and says, No, D. Garcia, no. She grips my jaw with ultimate authority, No, Garcia, no— and a minute later thrusts into kissing me, sucking furious as the wind races. And she's crazy, that young Berea, kissing the breath out of me with hot tongue, whispering gasps of, Fuck your mom. Suckles and bites and I respond, Your mom, Berea, and fuck your dad too; tugging at her golden curls and cursing her as she drops one hand and rips my zipper open in a fit, pulls me out and starts working me with her callused dish-wash long beauty fingers; lapping my lips, licking my tongue, my denim-clad hips pained with want, staggering in lust as the wind wags the spit bridge from our mouths; the open zipper teething my prick; as overhead, thick branches crack like deer rifles; as splinters plummet, as beneath our feet the black-green ground heaves and sinks and mushes.

And once more the Cause has confused us, has changed us has charged us straight into the sludge. And Berea drops down, down on the concrete ledge of the memorial to motherhood, her squat open-legged her cream knees a cradle as she fingers my belt loops and yanks down my jeans, first tasting me timidly and then sucking, ravenous, enraptured, pausing only to slobber and beseech, Please don't shame me, don't you shame me for this, D. Garcia. And I grip the headstone and say I will not and cannot, and then stare out into that collection of hyphenated used-to-be's and start bumping her wispy blond head into her own last name. Little American flags and plastic flowers, American American, my dear god, American, I clasp that granite and shove and dip, my hamstrings taut as she consumes me in pink gully cheeks, her pet noises and gags and muffled moans. The guitar drops off; I glance over to watch Pete, who is now jacking off and sobbing and half crouched behind a tombstone, his grip hand rabid as the other rubs his thinning hair; he stares at me, at my clenched, pumping ass, and within seconds casts ejaculate across a statuette of the white Virgin herself. I then turn back again to worship the dull pink lips that stretch and slide over me before Berea slip-spits me out and, Yes, she cries out, nearer thy God!; she strokes and strokes with hands so slick so tight so wet, her hands like a bolt-action rifle doused in gun oil, her eyes staring up into mine and the wind slapping my faith into submission; and, Come, she demands, Come now, baby, god she yanks so hard so slippery so, Come come come, and Make it real; she slides and grips and Okay, I say, oh kay oh . . . and my baptism erupts over herself and her dead mom.

And the clouds fracture into full torrent and flood, and the slop flows all around us. The slop like the slop in the desert in the void. The exhaust in the slop with the body oil and must as we rutted to our death through the gale in the desert. Only now, only here, the glass shards and bourbon vapors shove into mud as we slog away exhausted, and back to the car. Pebble hail plinks the metal roof like bamboo wind chimes; I crank the engine and then murder that accelerator, squealing out of the cemetery and over a nameless county road . . . whip-skid it through a four-way stop sign . . . and T-bone the side of a Chevy C-10 pickup with a worn metal camper over the bed.

Steam and furrowed metal, semen tang and pocked chrome; the droning, AM-drizzle of Conway Twitty's "I've Already Loved You in My Mind" from the truck cab; the driver, his head against the steering wheel, unshaven, his bulbous face all bloody but he's okay, I believe, from the register of disbelief in his algae-green eyes as I stumble by, staggering to the covered truck bed, towards the sounds of panic and foreign shushes.

Hail on metal. Mud-slug feet. Cold air in my open fly, I find six Mexicans jammed inside the camper—five women and a baby—smacked up and shivering and not a spackle of English, right there, in faded Wrestlethon t-shirts and Goodwill jeans, in ridiculous pain, praying to desiccate, invoking some resurrection of dust—instead of metal leaking sky-soaked, hand-muffled baby wails. Refugees now, they came so close to the end of some epic, or perhaps to the beginning of another, but got consumed by deluge in rust-truck Kentucky.

Surely, at least the baby's gonna be okay.

Maybe.

I think.

Laura died of the Black Plague, remember.

Hers

THEY FLEW US to the front in the belly of a loud C-130. We sat in cargo nets attached to the walls, bobbing in turbulence like babies in bouncer seats, too low to see out the windows. We landed in a gulf of dust and were jammed into trucks and taken to the compound, a small collection of tents inside a head-high berm of sand. A rocky desert horizon surrounded. We were ordered to calm down but stay sharp. Drink water.

Take chemical pills. Rumor was the pills were untested on humans, yet every morning we stood at parade rest, on the Iraqi border, in saggy, ill-fitting chemical suits, chewing the pills on command. It had been raining for days, so everything was soaked and beige and barren and slopped. (They had not briefed us on this wet climate. They had briefed us that Iraqis use American tanks and planes—we'd supplied them, after all—so the only way to discern the enemy was if he was firing on you.) The chem gear felt like a fatsuit as you lumbered around the compound, your boots sucked into the mud. A-10 Warthogs and F-whatever jets ripped the sky, unleashing their arsenal a few seconds north. Concussions from missile strikes buckled your knees, and shook you awake at night. Breathing meant wondering about sarin or VX asphyxia. A primary concern was whether your gas mask was truly airtight, or whether the atropine needle would break off in your femur when the time came to self-inject.

Take pills. Drink water.

Atropine: often fused with opiates, used to quell the death rattle.

After a week, one woman refused. She said her body was messing up because of the pills. Actually, she said "fucking up." She was African-American, late twenties, with short straightened hair. Thin legs but huge torso. She was ornery, and said fuck that because the pills were fucking her up.

Fine. She would die by Scud missile. They told us she was crazy, and told her, "Suit yourself." Another loud black chick with fat breasts and fried hair. I imagined her cruising the mall back in Tuscaloosa, talking loud, dragging a baby boy by his arm.

She refused the pills. A couple of weeks later she had to go to the medical tent. She wasn't pregnant—they knew *that* much. But her period had disappeared; she wouldn't bleed, and nobody could tell her why. The medical tent shipped her down to the battalion hospital, which shipped her down to the main hospital in Riyadh, which shipped her back up to camp to pack. "Mother *fuck*," she said. "All I wanted in this life was to serve, then to get home and start me a family. Now I can't even have no babies."

More tests were required. They sent her home. We never heard anything else.

◻   ◻   ◻

SPEC 4 Janette cried about her kid. You went to the motor pool to requisition a truck, ducked in the tent and saw the photo taped to her field desk: a tiny girl, towheaded, in a miniature Mississippi State cheerleader uniform. Don't ask if they'd taken her to the stadium on game day, or Janette would tear up and tell you about Colleen having fallen asleep during the Egg Bowl! She talked and cried while sitting near you at chow. Raised her voice to nobody at all about COLLEEN'S TURTLE DIED OH MAN WHY AM I NOT HOME? She missed her daughter while you ate breakfast, having just come off of guard duty. For hours you'd sat alone in a hutch at the edge of the compound, in the dark, facing the void through a slot between sandbags, your rifle aimed, your mind confabulating structures from the blackness. (Republican Guard advance or geometric patterns, the mind must see *something*.) You tried to forget that you'd traded your entire month's furlough for a ride in the back of a transport truck, breathing diesel exhaust and eating dehydrated pork, in order to wait in line for hours, to use a pay phone . . . to get your fiancée's answering machine.

And missiles burst. And the rains passed and the mud turned back to sand and windstorms engulfed everything for days, filling your boots, your eyes, your lungs, covering you in rashes. And Spec 4 Janette yapped and sobbed over her daughter, Colleen.

In our twelve-man tent, talk cycled about Janette's tight

workout body. One night, PFC Lomes tells everyone that during overnight guard duty he left his post to go smoke in the motor pool tent, and found Sergeant Cross pumping her. Says it just like this: "Sergeant Cross was pumping her, man. She had that good-hurt look on her face. Like, she was bent over her field desk, gripping the corners!" While telling us this he throws his hips like Sergeant Cross, grapples the air.

After lights-out, in the break between jet screams our tent was alive with fists rubbing against nylon sleeping bags. Everyone coming in silence.

CAMP was so small that Evie Mundleson and I saw each other every day. Yet she no longer spoke to me. Back in Riyadh, during in-processing, she had asked if I wanted to come with her. Had arched her eyebrows, and used the word *latrine*. By this point the females were no longer allowed makeup, so Evie's cheeks were a drama of settled red pocks. Her dye-blond hair had no benefit of product.

I had stared at her for a few seconds, then told her I had a fiancée.

"Oh. I'm sorry. It's just that, well."

It's just that everybody was fucking in the latrines. Port-o-lets labeled in Arabic whose plastic shells would rock and creak, whose sloshy reservoirs sounded like bathtub waves throughout the night. Just that we'd been stuffed inside a corrugated metal hangar outside Riyadh, were sweating, scared and unwashed, confined to ordered rows of olive-colored canvas cots and duffel bags. That Scud missiles traversed the night sky and the moon hung sideways. Half a million Iraqi troops were poised for the Mother of All Battles.

In-processing, in-country, at last. We had stared at each other for days. We had picked out the weaklings and placed bets against them. (Evie was the safest of the casualty bets.) We cleaned, then recleaned our carbines. Oiling the barrels, breaking down sight assemblies. They had known better than to issue us ammunition.

It's just that when not an activated reservist, Evie M. bar-backed at Game Day, a strip mall sports bar in north Tuscaloosa. There, her twenty-year-old body was losing to the free potato skins. Her nights were defined by Misty cigarettes, dead kegs, and tip-outs. And she was okay with this, there, between walls covered in Crimson Tide jerseys and plastic NASCAR flags. In Riyadh, at in-processing, she was scared beyond panic, shaking, wanting only to be groped in the community toilet. Many had felt the same.

WHEN by-the-book Sergeant Motes was sent home for being too old and sclerotic, Tetley Teabag and I became the de facto Supply and Armory leaders. Benefits included our very own tent, just Teabag and me. We bartered goods with other squads, companies, camps, armies, whomever. Extra boots got us a large, in-tent ice cooler; surplus cammies were good for foam mattresses; tent poles meant a radio, and so forth. We were sultans.

Tetley Teabag was a late-twenties rural Alabama high school graduate, desperate to be seen as a hardass. He had the mustache, buzz cut and accent, but was squat and soft and round. He also had the toe.

The Tetley Toe. Stateside, just before deployment, Tetley had thrust a posthole digger at the big toe of his left foot. This earned him an odd reattachment and a relentless wound. The medics made Tetley limp around on a so-called Chinese jump boot: an oversized medical shoe constructed of royal-blue canvas and white Velcro straps. The roughnecks harassed him for this, as did the officers, and the women.

But forget the boot. The thing about him was that he NEVER went to the showers. Night after night he shut the tent flaps and wiped himself clean with a wet rag. He called it a "bitch bath." In the dim orange lamplight, he'd turn his puppy-fat back to me and use this propane-powered camp stove to heat water in a tin basin. (By this point I was taking two-three-four cold showers a day. They kept drilling us for an attack that never came. The sand was everywhere. My lungs wheezed and my breath stank with it.) (This was also after Charlotte had stopped writing me.) As finale to Tetley's cleansing, he would wrap a Tetley tea bag around his blackened appendage. His grandmother sent boxes of them, instructing him that a woman's remedy was the only medicine a man could trust.

On guard duty one night I realized I'd forgotten my gas mask, and had to come back to the tent. Tetley was naked and bitch-bathing, and though he curled up when I cut through the entry flap, I saw what might be described as a mole or a nub, protruding from the thick beard between his legs.

I did not care that Tetley had the penis of an infant. Conversely, he seemed relieved to be uncloseted, because the next

night, during a violent sandstorm, he confessed to me that
he was a virgin. Said he was worried about dying unfulfilled.

"Mundleson is lonely," I yelled. We had to scream over the
wind. We lay on our cots with our goggles on and our mouths
covered by government-issue scarves. Rubbers were unrolled
over our gun barrels to keep the sand out. It was no use looking at each other because you couldn't see anything.

"What?"

"I bet Evie'd be your girlfriend," I shouted again.

"Screw that, man." He called her pug-ugly, which was
unfair, and which failed to trump that he could not expose
himself in theater. No two ways about it: the only way Tetley
could both keep his small penis a secret *and* lure a willing
partner was to get home alive and marry some Christian.

AFTER the nonmenstruating woman was sent away, only two
black girls remained. Back home they went to the U of A. One
of them, PFC Davis, had screwed this cheeseball Joe Minetti
in the toilet back at Riyadh. So there was *that*, and somehow
that had become attractive.

This, too, was after Charlotte stopped writing.

PFC Davis was inspiring. Curvy and defiant and laughing,
always sharp. One morning, the XO ordered the two women
and I to burn the latrine waste. He didn't say as much, but I
figured this was my punishment for hiding in the showers.
The black chicks did not have to figure anything. Our company was made up of Alabama rednecks and Spec 4 Janettes,
so they knew they'd just been born wrong.

We yanked large metal tubs from beneath seat-holes in the

plywood toilets, and burned what was inside. The tubs, having been half filled with diesel the week before, were brimhigh with turd and Tampax, vomit and ejaculate and toilet paper. And we lit all that on fire, and then walked from tub to tub, hour after hour, taking in putrid black smoke.

Diesel burns slow and won't explode when you light it. Nor will it penetrate the surface of the sewage. So you use a two-by-four to stir the char, to expose the flame to the sludge below.

Scorching shit in the desert. You get used to it. After a few hours, the three of us flirted around the feces. The sky was beige and gray. The sliver of landscape we saw over the compound berm was as barren as the moon.

"Y'all don't date black girls in y'alls fraternity?" Davis asked.

"Probably not," I said. "But I'm not against it."

"You sayin' you *have* dated a black girl?"

"Well, no. But I've thought about it."

"I bet you have." She laughed, then coughed.

She and I both knew a liaison would follow. She had overnight guard duty, alone, at the far corner of the berm. She said she needed company. I needed company.

Diesel will now and again race like gasoline. This happened as I was stirring a tub: a flame shot straight up the two-by-four, which I flung out of panic. It hit PFC Davis across the chest, smearing on her desert camo blouse.

"What tha hell was that, you?" she yelled.

"Sorry, sorry. Fire just jumped."

"You out of your goddamn mind?" She wiped her hands on me, then peeled off her soiled blouse and wiped that on me too. She was not wearing her required t-shirt and her breasts bulged from the top of her olive-green bra.

"Reaction," I said. "I—"

"What kinda man throws a flaming sticka shit at a woman?"

Both women cursed me and left for other fires. Though I tried to apologize several times, and soon bartered them both to the Frogs, neither spoke to me again.

This, in slow motion: the soiled board, twirling like a helicopter blade, aflame.

I strung up a large piece of cardboard across the tent wall behind my cot. I pinned photos on it of women I'd slept with, or whose pictures with me indicated that I might've. Drunken hugs at fraternity parties, suggestive poses, kisses on my cheek. These weren't the only photos I brought to combat. But after word got out that I'd spent a week on suicide watch in the medical tent, it became vital that I not be seen as a weak-ass, a Tetley.

Not pictured: Charlotte, in a royal-blue armchair near the window, dressed only in a white cotton shirt that was unbuttoned at the top. Sleeves gently rolled, her tan legs tucked under her on the wide chair cushion. I lay on the motel bed, naked except for dog tags. The windows were open, the transparent curtains billowed. She said we should look forward to being married when I got back. I did.

THEY dragged rank prisoners down the dirt road beside camp, like a slave march. They had stains on their pant asses and dust in their mustaches, and they begged us for the chewing gum and the salt packets from our MREs. Who knows where they went? Rumor was that they were nobodies, just a bunch of haji towelhead farmers, and we had better forget about them and get focused for the ground assault.

There was nothing happening. It was all outside the compound walls, staggering by, exploding in the distance.

MY grandmother wrote a letter in scrabbled blue ink. It was the first she had written since World War II, when my grandfather had done tours both in Europe and the Pacific. I do not know why she didn't send word to my father, in Vietnam.

When I was very young, going through a drawer I found an old black-and-white centerfold. Opening the trifolded paper, I was floored by this first glorious vision of sex. So much so that I did not recognize the subject. My mother walked in and caught me ogling, then nervously explained that she'd had her face superimposed on the body as a joke for my father when he was in combat.

Every day, every war, everybody waits for mail call.

AT some point, reborn from a psych eval down in Riyadh, I came to realize that war was more about dividends than killing. I needed a product. I started to make wine.

This old Choctaw cook had deep gulleys in his cheeks and when he spoke he emitted a soft whistle over the letter s: *sholdier, bishcuit, misshile.* He gave me a few packets of yeast, and taught me how to make applejack. Soon after, I was trading liters of it, alongside grapejack, orange-juice-jack and whatever-fruit-juice-I-could-get-jack, for fresh chicken and near-beer and battery-powered speakers.

One morning, a couple of French troops appeared. Not because they'd heard of my work as vintner, but because they needed a translator, and because one of the mechanics suspected that I might know a little French, being a college faggot and all. I cannot remember what the Frenchmen officially sought, but the next morning, in exchange for five gallons of my two-week-old applejack, an entire pallet of French rations was delivered to our tent. Tetley was angry. I told him to get ready for the Perrier.

The French meals came in tins, not brown plastic sacks. You didn't heat them by dropping floppy packets into warm water, you set the entire tin on Tetley's propane flame, then let the food baste in its own juices and herbs. Instead of dehydrated pork patty, this was *lapin avec haricots verts*.

"No shit, Tetley. It's rabbit, man. Bunny."

"No shit?"

"Yeah. And we got tons of bunny, man. Half yours too. You can bitch-bath in Perrier if you want."

This was, indeed, a moment. A fine moment. Cluster bombs, tracer rounds, intestinal parasites—*avec haricots verts*.

A five-gallon jug of bad wine was only worth a pallet of rabbit. The Perrier was traded for information about the location of the female sleeping quarters, when and where to cross over the berm, whether the women drank, if they were easy, etc. My French was better than I thought, and my answers worth an ocean of bubbling water.

The next morning we were ordered to a meeting with our

CO. He informed us that a bunch of drunk Frogs had spent the night in the women's tent. He said this was a war, not an orgy. Guard duty was redoubled. I was again ordered to latrine detail.

CHARLOTTE wrote that she was pregnant, that *we* were. Then she never wrote again. I burned shit in the desert and watched A-10s rip the sky.

The battalion colonel briefed us by saying that Intel had lost an Iraqi Special Forces unit in our area—So stay sharp, dogs. That night, I left my guard post, climbed over the berm and walked into the void. The red lens cover was on my flashlight; I aimed it forward and followed the circle. Day-bursts of missiles hit just up the road, briefly illuminating the blackness. I prayed for someone to fire on me as I neared the front. Nobody did. Darkness swallowed me, though the rocks and sand in the red circle of the flashlight vibrated with the missile strikes. I lay on the ground for a while to feel this, then put my ear against a large rock to listen to the sound. I got up and wandered for an hour or so, scouring that landscape. At some point I found a cluster of three tiny white flowers—the only living nature I'd seen for weeks. I yanked them, then went back to the tent and wrote Charlotte for the last time. I asked her to remember no matter what. To please make a list of details about me from back home, from before the war. I put the flowers in the envelope and was done.

▫   ▫   ▫

ONE sunset, some general helicoptered in, gave us a ten-minute speech about victory, then left. He had a slight gut but strong posture, and he walked back and forth in his beige cammies as the red sun melted down behind him. We never saw him again, but he made clear that we would lead the invasion, would spearhead a 155-mile thrust into Baghdad, "crushing any rag-wrapped cunt" who got in our way.

Every vehicle was armored. We sandbagged the Deuce-and-a-Half truck beds; we welded metal plates on the doz-ers and dumps. We jury-rigged a .50-cal mount on a pickup cab and pretended to know how to use it.

They said, Go.

For a mute instant there was no gender. We charged north, trucks and guns, past missile craters, charred vehicles and burned trash. It was apocalyptic and eerie, abandoned, but we scanned the desert eagerly, looking back and forth to find the enemy at last.

We located a collection of goatskin-covered foxholes, and exited the trucks. Our rifles set on three-round semiautomatic burst, we stalked up with gun stocks to our cheeks. The holes were empty save for Arab pinups and empty water bottles and cigarette butts. The airplanes had done all the killing. We pushed on, north, so very much in search of death.

The convoy drove for hours on the same scab of earth, no enemy in sight, our own tracks disappearing behind us in sand drift. At some point the combat-support vehicles just stopped.

They radioed us and said to turn around. The war was over.

We got out of the trucks in the middle of Iraq and took our helmets off. We yelled and unloaded our rifles, ejaculating brass casings all over the desert. Yet the silence was unbreakable.

THE next day, Tetley and I were ordered to make a supply run and find a victory feast. We cruised the desert highway, a crisp gray seam of asphalt through the beige landscape. Out of nowhere, an enormous cloud of sand rose ahead of us. Tetley drove us straight toward it, an oncoming, massive armament convoy. Flitting strips of red, white and blue nylon tied to tank antennae against the grainy Arabian sky.

On the shoulder to our right I saw a camel. She sat there, buckled down on all fours, groaning. To our left, soldiers stood up in the beds of transport trucks, whooping and dancing and grabbing their crotches. Pop music blared, brakes squealed. The convoy trucks were sluggish and clumped together, billowing the enormous sand cloud. Armed Forces Radio announced total victory; President Bush declared an end to the Vietnam era.

A thin film of sand coated the camel's black eyes and crusted her eyelashes. The troops, many shirtless, their silver dog tags wagging, yelled and waved, and danced, the exhaust stacks spewing and horns blaring, the music cranked from boom boxes. All of it, us, charging east-west in a horde along an unmarked two-lane in the desert.

Next to the camel was her calf. It had tire tracks on its belly and a bunch of bloody black gut-ropes shooting out its ass. I was amazed at how precisely indented the tread grooves were on the tiny rib cage. Tetley never saw this. I looked over and watched him pump his fist at the soldiers, and I didn't say anything. We passed the camels, the female's head cocked upwards, her eyes staring at me, her mouth open, bleating.

WHEN we started to break camp, Saudi farmers loitered outside the compound, lured by our discarded plywood and burlap and such. Given their gestures and keyword English, we determined that they wanted to use the scraps to repair animal hutches, make sheds and so forth. Do whatever it is farmers do with wood and corrugated metal. Hour after hour, days in the sun, the men stood there, white robes and red-checked headscarves. They grinned and mock-saluted, standing just beyond the compound wall next to their tiny white Datsun trucks.

We were ordered to give them nothing. Haji bastards are tricky, our commanders said. You never know what kind of weapon can be fashioned from canvas or particleboard.

After a few days, the farmers brought their daughters out to greet us. Not kids, not sons, but daughters, head to foot in black robes, bearing the wind like polluted ghosts. Waving at us. When this had no effect, the daughters were made to remove their veils. They prostituted smeary lipstick smiles. (One of the guys who talked to them swore it was house paint, not makeup.) Still, we hauled all of the usable materials out, passing them by, diesel exhaust and catcalls from truck cabs, en route to the burn site.

Tremendous pyres dotted the desert expanse in all directions. Streaks of black smoke rose into the sky. Tents, tarps, plywood scraps; Meals Ready to Eat, water jugs, candy wrappers, tires, extra uniforms . . . All of it was stacked into large pyramids and set on fire.

The farmers still stood there, waiting. We tried to run them off. Their enthusiasm waned but they still smiled, smiled and waved when you took stuff to be burned, and we couldn't look at them anymore, and we yelled at them, or just waved and smiled and said, "Hi, haji fuckface," or whatever, or swerved the truck at them just a little bit, just enough to get them to jump back. We flicked our tongues at their daughters. We spat.

Alongside the order to burn, we had orders that every single grain of sand be removed from every single piece of equipment: dozers, pans, back-end loaders, trucks, etc. By no means would we be bringing home any Holy Land. They built a massive parking lot in the middle of the desert, then parked hundreds of vehicles there, in rows. With the pyres littering the landscape around us, we washed sand off of things.

Evie Mundleson and I were ordered to scour the ambulance with power sprayers. The vehicle had never been used, so the detail was a joke. We opened the bay doors and sprayed the metal walls and the metal bunks and the open metal shelving. Sandy water poured onto the ground, alongside three black scorpions.

I walked over, kicked the scorpions around for a minute. Laughed while they pinched at my boot.

"Come on, man," she said, then stomped on them.

I asked her if she was excited to go home.

"No way. You?"

"Nope."

□   □   □

LAST stop was Khobar Towers, a residential building complex outside Riyadh. In the courtyard between the high-rises the Army leashed up a camel. You could pay $5 for a Polaroid with it. They set up vending, bad pepperoni pizza and non-alcoholic beer, and kiosks sold cheap Saudi souvenirs, prayer rugs and t-shirts. There was a pool.

Amid the thousands in that sober Araby I ran across D. Garcia, this skinny Mexican I'd grown tight with during Basic Training at Fort Jackson. An Army truck driver, D. Garcia had logged over a million miles in theater. I told him I only wanted to be back in that sand. He said he just wanted to be back on that highway.

That night—the last time I would ever see him—D. Garcia and I falsified a requisition for a transport truck, a Deuce-and-a-Half, and stole into some immigrant area of the city, Filipino, where he'd discovered you could buy black market rotgut. It was nasty and clear and came in plastic water bottles. We got drunk and skidded all over back-alley Riyadh, screaming out of the open windows of the truck cab.

Back at Khobar we staggered through the hallways, playing commando. We gave hand signals like in the movies, and then snuck into rooms. There, Garcia aimed his fingers at sleeping troops, mock-fired several rounds, then stepped back into the hall and on to clear the next quarters.

Behind one door we found the women, splayed out on cots, sleeping in Army-green panties, a thin layer of sweat on their exposed skin. Evie Mundleson was among them, asleep on her chest, shirtless, her breasts all smushed out. D. Garcia cocked his eyebrow at me, raised the barrel of his finger-gun to the roof, motioned for me to go inside. I nodded. He pointed two fingers at his eyes, and then at me, and then disappeared forever. I saw myself stumble over to Evie; I heard the moan that would erupt as I yanked down her battlefield panties and shoved it all straight up her ass.

I still don't know what stopped me. Really, there was no barrier left. No ethic, no cause. Yet I'm pretty sure I just went back to my bunk, jerked off in silence.

FAMILIES and cameras on the tarmac at Bragg. It was hot and humid, and Charlotte was not there, though I couldn't stop looking for her. People hugged people, hugged children, hugged reporters. Every hand waved those little American flags you find in the cemetery. Someone handed out Southwest Asia Service Medals.

That night we put a bunch of bottles together, tequila, Jägermeister, Jack, what have you. It was guys-only. Everyone brought a fifth of the liquor they'd missed most. We drank violently, sitting on the patio outside the barracks, our dog barks reverberating off the concrete into the warm southern evening. We piled in a minivan cab and went to town. The driver didn't even ask, "Where to?" He just dumped us on a busy, soldiered street full of bars. We wandered among hundreds of redeployed troops, amid loud music and vendors and neon. A barker talked us into one of the endless nasty clubs.

Cigarettes and air freshener and terrible music. A brown-skinned woman in a denim miniskirt and halter top marched up, and I asked her for a beer. She said nothing, only yanked me to the back of the room as the guys howled. She pulled me behind a partition, lifted her halter, placed my hands on her large breasts, then put her own hands over mine and began rubbing us in circles. It made me think of a Laundromat.

"You like these tits?" she asked.

"Uh-huh," I answered. She might have been Mexican. She walked me into a small room with a lamp and an olive-colored military cot. I had to put both hands on the wall to hold myself up as she undid my pants and put a condom over me. She sat on the cot and started to work me over like a machine, licking my anus for a few seconds, mouthing my testicles, fellating me just enough to promote erection. Straight-up checklist: hike miniskirt, panties to ankles, bend over. Enfranchise me with hard statements about my masculinity as I penetrate. I finished instantly but tried to keep going, accidentally lodging the condom inside her after I went limp. I handed her all my money, then stumbled into a bathroom stall and wept.

IN Tuscaloosa I borrowed a pair of eyeglasses from a friend, pulled a Crimson Tide ball cap low on my brow, and went to see Charlotte, unannounced. I had never worn glasses, so everything was blurry. My clothes felt borrowed and dated, and were musty from a year in the drawer. She answered the door and we stood there, silently, until finally she said she was glad to see me. She was sorry how things had worked out.

It had just rained and was July-hot. There was no baby. You could smell that the box hedges outside her apartment had just been clipped. I had not reacclimated to southern humidity and a constellation of zits had erupted on my face. I asked if she wanted to go to the zoo or something. I cannot remember if we went. I really have no idea.

I am positive, however, that the next time I saw her it was twelve years later, far from Alabama. We ran into each other at the edge of the frozen fish section at Costco Wholesale, in Chicago, Illinois. Another George Bush was President, and a new war in the same desert was cracking wide open. And there she was.

Only, I wasn't nineteen. I was a grown man. One of thousands who'd been slowly drawn away. Away from fathers who fought in better wars, from male friends whose only interest was whether or not these men had killed anyone. From churches in small southern towns where they were made to stand on Veterans Day. Instead of the VFW or the VA, this crybaby diaspora sought out spaces both alien *and* familiar: exurb, highway, divorce court, Costco. These were grown men who shopped for discount liquor in bulk. Grown men whose doctors could not explain the sensation of fire beneath the skin. Men who could not pin their failed relationships on anything quantifiable, who obsessed over the inability to recover the lives they saw on TV. A grown man in a beige suede jacket that had lost its nap, and who had spent the many previous days on the floor of his efficiency apartment, watching a new invasion unfold on a small television. Missile strikes at remove, rabbit ears adjusted, a rerun that somehow eclipsed the original. He showered and sobbed and masturbated.

Nobody ever asks about the grown women.

Charlotte was still pretty and soft-spoken, though now

with a master's and a career, and the confidence to look squarely at the past. We stood under the fluorescence, smiling past each other, eyeballing bulk packages of cod, scrod, halibut. I wondered if she had made or kept that list, the one detailing who I was before the war.

She got my phone number before I could ask for hers, and she said we should get a cup of coffee.

Of course, she never called.

"Why on earth would we ever go back?" was the last I ever heard.

ACKNOWLEDGMENTS

To Dana Lee and Virginia Philomena, with everything I've got. To my wonderful family, Lindsey and Whiting and DeMasi and DeLoca. To Bill Clegg. To Jill Bialosky. To Liz Birch and Brendan McGrath, Allan B. "Preacher" Hunt, Kyle Beachy, Chris Bower, Thomas D'Angelo and Caitlan Mackinnon-Patterson, Werllayne Nunes and Molly Dondero, Lee Eastman II, Alice Randall, David Metcalf and Erin Moody, Margaret Patton Chapman and Tony Strimple, Richard Holland, Ken MacLeish and Rachael Pomerantz, Andrew Mullins, Justin McGuirk, Maggie Tate, Robert Rea, Cale Nicholson. . . . To Robert Olen Butler, Chris Clemans, Maria Rogers, Michael Strong. To Lynelle Keil, Scott Gray, and the Pals who visit Willow Street in Austin. To John and Angela Young, Rob Harrington, Carter Little, and My Extended Nashville Comrades. To Ted Ownby, Ann Abadie, Jimmy Thomas, and the staff at the Center for the Study of Southern Culture, University of Mississippi. To Sara Levine and everyone at the MFA in Writing, School of the Art Institute of Chicago. To the Tennessee Arts Commission, the Sewanee Writers' Conference, and the Center for Medicine, Health, and Society at Vanderbilt. To Square Books. To the *Iowa Review*, and the Jeff Sharlet Memorial Award for Veterans. To all y'all, with a thanks that feels broken, because a word like thanks doesn't even come close.